Loving You

SECOND ACT
BOOK THREE

KATIE BINGHAM-SMITH

Copyright © 2024

All rights reserved.

No part of this publication may be reproduced, distributed, or transmitted in any form or by any means, including photocopying, recording, or other electronic or mechanical methods, without the prior written permission of the publisher, except as permitted by U.S. copyright law.

The story, all names, characters, and incidents portrayed in this production are fictitious. No identification with actual persons (living or deceased), places, buildings, and products is intended or should be inferred.

All brand names and product names used in this book are trademarks, registered trademarks, or trademarks of their respective holders. Philigry Publishing is not associated with any product or vendor in this book. For permission requests, contact Katie Bingham-Smith at katie@katiebingham-smith.com.

To never giving your power away.

CHAPTER 1
Abby

"It's so strange having someone else do my hair. I love it." Grace, one of the stylists from the Beauty Bar, gives my long, blond waves a final spray. I haven't liked the way I look this much since my twenties. It's sad that it's taken something like my friend Ivory's wedding to stop long enough to let someone pamper me.

"You're a professional forty-five-year-old woman, Abby. You deserve to get your hair done more than once every six months."

"No offense, Grace, that's easy for you to say with your handy husband and no kids and all that," Lila chuckles. Large curlers cover her head, and even though she hasn't even had her makeup done yet, she's flushed and glowing, like she spent the weekend in a tropical sunny place. I narrow my eyes on my friend. I love her, and I'm jealous because if I didn't know better, I'd say she just had sex.

I sigh. I guess that's what being in love does to you, gives you that glow that annoys every single woman on earth. Even the women who want the best for you.

Grace gives her the finger, and the two of them laugh. There's no offense taken, and I love how we can all tell it like it is and not worry about ruffling each other's feathers. "You're both so lucky to have a friend like me who puts up with you and offers to do your hair. What with my life of luxury and all. I'm happy to help you two poor single moms."

Grace is a great listener, and incredibly generous. In the year I've been working at the salon, she always asks me if I want a cut, highlight, or Brazilian Blowout. As much as I want to take her up on it, I'm always running from one thing to the next. My daughter's basketball games, heading home to meet some crusty handyman who's repairing the front steps that have rotted, or getting the oil changed on the car. Meeting Mr. Voyeur who messaged me this morning asking, again, if I could find a friend with benefits to blow while he watched.

Grace is right. I can make more time for my hair and less time for useless men. But fuck, doing life alone, especially around the holidays, sucks. There are days when I'm not sure how I'm going to pull it off. Nights I can't fall asleep, wondering if I'll be able to save enough for Stella's college bills, wondering if I'll trust another man again after Ben's affair.

My self-induced pity party is over when Ivory emerges from the bathroom, her veil cascading behind her silk ivory dress like spun sugar.

Lila, Grace, and I turn to face her. I'm breathless. Not only does Ivory look stunning with her blond hair in a loose bun at the nape of her neck, but she's so completely *Ivory*. She and Rome fit together like two puzzle pieces, and my heart aches with how much I want what they have.

"You look so amazing," I say, tears pooling in my eyes.

"You really do," Grace and Lila say in unison.

Our makeup artist, Brett, waves a big brush through the air. "See ladies, this is why I wait until after you see the bride to do your makeup. Now wipe your eyes, it's time for me to make your lashes as black as your hearts, you little vixens."

Three hours later, I'm standing in the corner hiding behind one of the bare birch trees that's adorned with lights, eating a piece of chocolate wedding cake in my hands because I can't be bothered with a damn fork.

Everything about this night has been perfectly magical for my friends. Rome cried as he and Ivory exchanged vows, then I got to watch Lila and Holt slow dance with his hand on her ass the entire time. I'm trying to dig into the deep parts of my brain that keep telling me I'm better than to be jealous of my friends, but it's not quite working.

This enormous barn has been transformed into a snow globe. Large gold disco balls hang from the wooden beams that are covered in garlands, and each long buffet table is draped with a white tablecloth. Candles running down the length of the tables glow, illuminating the dim room, and each guest was presented with a little white box tied with a gold ribbon. Inside was a tiny crystal Christmas tree ornament.

When I opened mine, I kept my head down. Watching my ornament catch flickers of light felt a lot better than observing all the couples opening their decorations together, holding them up to the large chandelier hanging from the cathedral ceiling, huge smiles on their faces. I could sense every single one of them though.

I know today is about Ivory, but when you're single, events like this make it hard to focus on anything else other than your own loneliness.

I have my daughter Stella, and my parents have been so supportive since my divorce. I love my job, and my little house. My life is full. But my heart feels empty. I know society tells me I can do it all; handle life on my own without a man.

But what if I don't want to? What if I want a man? I want someone to do life with. Someone to hold me at night. Someone to give foot rubs to. Someone to order a pizza with every Friday.

Now that Stella is sixteen and doesn't need me as much, I have space to take care of another person. As long as they take care of me too, of course. Lord knows I'm a handful, but I have a lot of love to give.

A shiver runs down my spine when I sense I'm being watched. I look around the barn as couples sway and the waitstaff starts clearing away plates and silverware, the scent of bacon, scallops, and maple syrup from dinner still in the air.

It's not until I look to my left that I see a tall man coming toward me. The closer he gets, the clearer I can see his strong jaw and clean-shaven face. He's dressed all in black and wearing an apron, definitely not much older than thirty. He probably caught me taking this second piece of cake and is going to call me out on it. He smirks and interlocks his hands behind his back when he reaches me. "I couldn't help but notice you."

Just when I think he's going to scold me for taking another hunk of cake before some people haven't even had their first, his eyes run over my body.

My breath catches, and I scan the room. No one is behind me, or even close to us. Is this gorgeous boy-man checking me out? Two dimples appear, and his biceps are pushing at his sleeves. I meet his eyes again and straighten before dropping the piece of cake on my plate like I wasn't just making out with it in a dark corner.

"I'm Matthew. I've been watching you all night. If I wasn't working this event, I would've had your number in my phone hours ago. In fact, I'd be sending you a flirty text right now." He pulls his phone from his back pocket. "I have to get back to work, but I'd love to take you to dinner. Or have you for dinner."

Is this really happening? Maybe all I've needed to do this whole time is eat a piece of cake with my hands behind a tree to attract a man. Screw the dating sites. This is way better. "Yes, I'd like that. My name is Abby," I say like this complete stranger didn't just offer to pleasure me orally.

"Hello, Abby," he says, those dimples making my stomach dip.

Keep your cool. Be chill. You are so chill. I grab his phone and enter my number. Handing it to him, I say, "Now get back to work, Matthew." Maybe it's not such a good idea. His fuckboy scent is stronger than the smell of bacon wafting through the air, but fuck it, I don't care. This was a wonderful night, but a rough one. And thinking of a gorgeous man with his head between my thighs inspires me, even if I am setting myself up for another mess. Something I've gotten really good at.

My chest is alive with thousands of butterflies, and I resist the urge to giggle as he tips his chin and says, "I'll be talking with you soon, Abby."

Or eating me soon, I want to say, but keep the thought buried inside as I watch him saunter away. He rakes his hand through his dark hair, a tattoo peeking from his shirt collar. I tilt my head, a devilish smile tugging at my lips. *And that will soon be your view during your next orgasm.*

Just like that, my pity party's over. I guess you never know when the energy is going to change. Or when a delicious man is going to catch you eating cake and offer to do some munching of his own.

Filling my lungs with air, I feel amazing as I dump the rest of the cake in the trash then head to the bathroom. I'm going to freshen up, and get out on that dance floor for the last dance of the evening. Sultry Abby has kicked Pitiful Abby out of the building.

As I approach the restroom, my thighs rubbing together under two pairs of Spanx I'm going to peel off as soon as I can, I think I hear Matthew's voice. My steps slow, I don't want him to think I'm following him. I mean, I totally would meet him in the bathroom so he could make good on his offer, but even then, I'm not going to *run* after him. Although that buzz cut and tattoo is worth a power walk for sure.

"Ha! Dude, I got it!" he bellows. And I giggle thinking how cute it is that he's bragging to his friends.

I take another step closer to the kitchen entrance. "I got that blond's number. Give me my fifty bucks!" My face heats and I feel the cake I just shoved in my mouth rising in my chest. I hold the wall for support, everything in me telling me I should just walk away and not listen to the rest of this, but I freeze.

"Shut up, she's old enough to be your mom. I can't believe she fell for it. Does she actually think you're going to call? Pathetic!"

This feels like a bad dream, like I'm about to listen to someone point out all the things I hate about myself. I have no idea who Matthew is talking to, it must be another kid working the kitchen, but I'm absolutely mortified. I'm an idiot to think a young, hot man would be interested in someone like me: a middle-aged woman eating wedding cake like it can actually fill the gaping hole in my heart.

"Oh yeah, she does. Like giving candy to a baby. I should have told her to lay off the cake. Her ass is—"

I cover my ears and run to the parking lot, my black wristlet hitting me in the side of my face as I do. I can't do this. I can't be here. Not even for my best friends. I've had enough tonight. Maybe I am being selfish and maybe I should stay for Ivory, but I can't do this for another second.

I'm pathetic, broken. Before I know it, I'll be fifty, Stella will be gone and I'll be alone, and yes, I'll still have a big ass and thick thighs. They've been a part of me since I was twelve, and they're obviously not going anywhere.

When I start my car, I realize I've left my coat inside. Not even the frigid December air can get me back in that barn. Stella is at a sleepover, and I can go home and cry in the bathtub as long as I want. It certainly won't be the first time.

CHAPTER 2
Abby

"I'm so glad you could fit me in, dear. I was worried when Ivory told me she'd be on her honeymoon, then off until Christmas. I need my hair done for the holidays, you see. I'll be so busy baking my famous cinnamon rolls for friends, family, and well, half the state really, I'll barely have time to sleep."

I stand behind Marge, at least that's what I think her name is, and say, "Of course. Feeling your best during the holidays is a must," before turning on the blow dryer because I can't talk anymore. My positivity has almost run out for the day, and I need to keep whatever's left for Stella.

I've somehow fit in a handful of Ivory's regular clients, who were so distraught she would be taking two weeks off before Christmas, on top of my own. Of course I had to do it for her. Ivory cares about her customers a little more than I do if I'm being honest, and well, I care about Ivory a lot. She's saved my ass more than once since I'm constantly late to work. Oh, then there was the time I completely forgot I told one of my regulars I'd come in at six in the morning to do her highlights. Ivory got her started then called to remind me. When I burst into the Beauty Bar, a crumpled mess without makeup, apologizing all over the place, Ivory smiled and said, "I was here anyway, it's no problem. She wasn't even upset." Even if my customer was mad, Ivory never would've told me. Her magical way of handling hard things is as rare as a good man, and definitely a quality I don't have.

My feet are still aching from the heels I wore to Ivory's wedding. Four inches was a bit aggressive, but I love what they do for my thighs and ass. Not to mention I was feeling feisty that night, hoping I'd meet someone other than the asshole who should've left me to my chocolate cake.

I swivel Marge's chair sideways, then glance at my reflection. I like my bubbly ass and strong thighs. I'm not afraid to wear leggings or tight skirts, and that little waiter boy wouldn't know what to do if his head was between my luscious legs anyway.

Trying to stay busy all weekend to keep from feeling sorry for myself, and to forget about how hard I cried when I got home from the wedding didn't totally work. Yes, he's an idiot, but I can still hear his voice, can still see him walking away from me as I stood alone in the corner, believing that he was actually feeling me.

Maybe I should ask Marge if she knows anyone I could date? Sure, she's in her sixties, but maybe she's got a single friend or a brother. An older man, preferably a rich one, is exactly what I need. Yes! Why haven't I ever thought about that before? These bozos I've been dating lack the emotional maturity I need in my life. I might as well go for money.

As I roll the brush through her hair, lost in thought, Marge closes her eyes and that makes me smile. I may be scattered and always running late, but I do love making women feel their best. I've been self-absorbed today, and yes I'm tired from working twelve-hour days, but I can rest later. Like when Stella is grown and gone. Hopefully, by that time, I won't still be panicking every month about making the mortgage payment. Or still be single and alone. Oh fuck, I better not be alone.

Marge's hands are folded in her lap, and the stack of diamond rings on her left hand makes my heart skip a beat. How long has she been married? Has she only been married once? Is he the love of her life? Did her husband ever cheat on her, or tell her no one would want her when she decided to leave his cheating ass like Ben did to me?

When I turn off the hairdryer and slide it into my drawer, a wave of panic runs through me when the song, "Miss You Most (at Christmas Time)" hums through the speaker. The Beauty Bar is lively for a Monday night, everyone talking and laughing. The holiday magic is alive, and it makes me wonder how much longer I'll be ... in this place, feeling sorry for myself desperately trying to pull myself out of it, only to land in the exact same spot.

I haven't even had the time to get a tree or start my Christmas shopping. The thought of doing it alone turns my stomach. I want to crawl into bed and stay there until after the New Year. I officially suck.

I have to pull it together for Stella. Yes, she's around to help me put up and decorate the tree, but she's not as present as she was when she was little. Her friends and that damn phone have become way more important than spending quality time with me, which is just the way it goes, but I don't have to like it.

My parents would help me get ready for the holidays like they did last year, but I don't want to ask them for another thing. They've helped me so much since my divorce, and my older sister, Rebecca, made a comment at Thanksgiving about me being a forty-five-year-old woman-child. I should've kicked her under the table like I used to when we were kids, but then I'd just be proving her right. Must be nice to have a surgeon for a husband and two homes. Although Stan is never around anymore and Rebecca comes to all the family functions alone. No wonder she's so miserable. Not that I should talk. Although I'm pretty sure I get laid more than she does.

I separate Marge's hair into sections and smile at her reflection in the mirror. "How do you like the color? It's a bit darker than your usual."

"Oh, I just love it. I look fabulous, don't I?" Her light blue eyes twinkle as she tousles her bangs.

"You absolutely do."

"Max, my husband, is going to feel like he's with another woman tonight."

Marge waggles her eyebrows, and I laugh. I really want to be Marge when I grow up. If I ever do.

"Can I ask you something, Marge?"

"Ask me anything, dear. I'm old and know almost everything." Marge's legs are crossed, and she swings her foot as twist a section of hair around the curling iron.

"How long have you and Max been married?"

"Forty years last week! Can you believe I'm old enough to say that? You want to know the secret to staying together for that long?"

I release her hair, then grab my comb to tease the next section of her shoulder-length bob. "I do, yes. I was married once. Maybe I would've stayed that way if I knew your secret."

"Good sex!" Marge blurts out as everyone in the salon turns toward her. "Now I know you probably think senior citizens don't do it anymore, but they most certainly do. Why every Monday, Wednesday, and Friday, Max and I have our special time." Marge looks around, shaking her pointer finger like she's teaching a class. "It's very important. When you're not having sex, it's a huge deal."

I force a smile, Marge's words cutting through me. Ben used to say that and said that was the reason he fucked the new secretary from his office. It's so cliche I want to punch him every time I think about it. I didn't feel sexual for years after having Stella, and he never asked me what was wrong or seemed to give a shit that I was working full-time weeks after her birth, and I was the only one who got up with her at night so he could sleep.

After a while he stopped trying, and I was so relieved.

I never want that to happen again, I will prioritize sex! But I didn't know it'd be this hard to find a relationship after a divorce *and* have all the great sex. Which is why I've settled for breadcrumbs and false promises from men I meet online. Men I don't really like. Except for Mr. Voyeur.

As much as I know that can't continue and I already told him I couldn't see him again, my heart flutters when I think about calling him later to see if he's available in a few nights while Stella is with her dad. *Don't do it. Don't go backward. Besides, you're too busy for a man right now. Maybe after Christmas you'll get back out there ...*

"Well, that's great advice. And you're right it is important. I let that part of my marriage go. Never again." I shake my head and purse my lips.

"Well, dear there were two of you in your marriage. The man has to do his part too. If only men these days knew how important it was for a woman to feel safe, to be listened to, to be noticed. Instead, they're ignoring their spouse, sliding into DMs hoping for some kind of attention from other women instead of tending to their business."

"Marge!" I say under a laugh. "And you know this because?"

"Oh please, I get messages quite often. Men like to test the waters even though they know I'm married. Just the other day I posted a selfie in my new Christmas sweater on Instagram and, well here"—Marge takes her phone from her purse and her finger slides over the screen—"I showed these to Max, but

I got three messages. One from a high school friend. Another from the man who owns the drugstore downtown. I go in there with Max all the time, he knows I'm married. It didn't stop him from sending three fire emojis though!"

I shake my head, trying not to laugh. Marge sounds disgusted at these men, but she's clearly enjoying herself as she continues to talk about how she's not going to stop posting pictures of herself to stop all the "unwanted attention" she's getting. She's so entertaining, just the distraction I need, that I almost ignore my buzzing phone. It's almost seven, and I'll be done and headed home soon, but I check the screen to make sure it's not Stella.

"Excuse me, I want to hear more about this, but my daughter is home alone and I want to make sure she's all right."

"Of course, dear. Just wait until you hear what Tim said. His wife died last year, and he likes the younger ladies."

"Oh yes, I don't want to miss what Tim said." My heart sinks when I read Stella's text: *Mom, the freaking washing machine is broken or something. There's water all over the floor.*

I grip my phone, willing the tears to stay in my eyes until I get in my car later. I'm so depleted. I don't even have the energy to get ready for the damn holidays, meanwhile everyone else has their tree, perfect hair, and are getting messages from men across the state after posting a damn Christmas sweater selfie.

Marge places her hand on my arm. "Oh, what is it, dear? You look like you might be sick. Is your daughter okay?"

I slide my phone back into my purse and try to take a deep breath. "She is, thank you. But I'm not. My washing machine is broken and flooding my laundry room and I feel like I'm going to break in two." I don't even care how unprofessional I'm being right now. The salon is spinning, the fumes from hairspray make me feel like I might pass out. Or throw up. Or get in my car and drive until I run out of gas because I can't do life right now.

"Oh, hang on. My nephew, Dylan, has an appliance repair business. I'll call him right now, dear. We'll get him to your house. What's your address?"

CHAPTER 3
Dylan

My spine feels like it might crack in two after all the appointments I had today. Fuck, pulling out that ancient, water-filled washer from the wall to get behind it and see what the hell was going on was the death of me. Backbreaking work knows no age. It's a good thing I love what I do because when my Aunt Marge called and put me on speakerphone with Abby, who obviously had an emergency, just as I was unwrapping my sandwich and settling in for the night, I couldn't exactly say no.

Abby is a single mom, Christmas is weeks away, and I can't exactly leave her with a flooded laundry room and a washing machine that doesn't work. I could tell by the desperation in her voice that she was on the verge of tears. It tugged at my heart. I was raised by an amazing single mom, and I've never met my dad. I don't even know if he's even still alive. Mom always told me we were better off without him, and for the most part, I believed her.

But those nights I'd hear her pace the floor as I lay in bed, our dog Cooper at my feet, I couldn't help but wonder if we really were better off without a man in the house. She never seemed interested in men, said that I was her focus and she wasn't about to waste her time and energy on anything else but me and work.

Even as a young kid I wanted more for her even though I never found the right words to tell her that. Mom worried about money a lot. Her two waitressing jobs always put food on the table, and her best friend's husband was a mechanic who kept her old Dodge running.

But if something went wrong with the house, whether it was an appliance, a leaky roof, or a clogged drain, we would try to fix it together. We usually figured it out. By the time I was a sophomore in high school, I'd accepted the fact I was the man of the house.

A year and a half after that, Mom was diagnosed with brain cancer. That's when I decided to start my business as an appliance repairman. I loved taking things apart, figuring out what was wrong, then putting them back together. Part of that had to do with wanting to figure out what parts were making mom sick, removing them, and making her good as new. But when her doctor gave her less than a year to live, all I could focus on was making her comfortable and happy for her last few months.

All my friends were headed to college the year I started Applied Appliance Repairs, but it didn't bother me. I hated sitting in a classroom anyway. My teachers tried to get me to apply to a few schools, reassuring me that my grades would probably get me a full ride to the University of Maine.

I got enough money for graduation to run a few ads and word of Applied Appliance got around fast. Before I knew it, I was booked out for a month. Then six months. That was nine years ago, and I haven't regretted it. Not even on nights like tonight when I'd like nothing more than to eat my cold dinner and pass out on the sofa in my underwear. I make a great living, every day is different, and I'm happy which is a hell of a lot more than most of the men I know, my age and older. Plus, I know Mom is looking down on me every day, so proud of the man I've become.

Abby doesn't live too far away, and the twenty-minute ride got me in the Christmas spirit. The seat warmer in my truck did wonders for my stiff back which is always a plus. And there's nothing like listening to carols as you drive through the quaint little towns in Maine right before the holiday. If I wasn't in such a hurry to get to Abby's house and access the water damage, I would've driven slower like I usually do. There's something about going for a drive at night and seeing all the Christmas trees twinkling through the windows, and wreaths on front doors with a dusting of snow that makes memories of Mom more vivid.

The first few Christmases after she was gone, I didn't even acknowledge this time of year. It was too painful. But she wants me to remember the Christmas mornings we spent by the woodstove, exchanging handmade gifts before making French toast together.

I pull into Abby's driveway and jog to the front door. There's no sign of Christmas to be found as I peek through her windows and knock on the light green front door. The outdoor lights are turned on, giving the cedar shake cottage a cozy feel, and my lips curl into a smile when my eyes fall to the doormat that says, "Home: where the Ho & Me come together."

A wide-eyed teenager wearing shorts and a sweatshirt rips the door open. "Thank God you're here before Mom. She's going to low-key freak out when she sees the laundry room."

I hope it's not as bad as she says it is. If there's one thing that's hard for me to watch is a woman freaking out, low-key or not, whatever the hell that means. But that's why I'm here.

To hopefully prevent a meltdown and get Abby's washing machine up and running.

"I'm here to help. I'm Dylan by the way." I set down my tool box and slide a pair of disposable booties over my boots. Scanning the small open space, I see dirty dishes are waiting in the sink, and there are blankets, pillows, and a few books in a pile on the worn-in leather sofa. Piles of mail sit next to the stove, and while the home isn't dirty, it's a little cluttered and smells like maple syrup.

"I'm Stella," she replies over her shoulders as her slippered feet scuff across the living room then down the hall.

I follow her, and when Stella stands in the doorway of the laundry room, heaps of towels, sweatshirts, and jeans to the right of the washer, she pulls out her scrunchie and redoes her messy bun. "I turned off the washing machine and mopped up all the water." Her eyebrows are raised as if to ask, "What are we going to fucking do?"

It's now my job to calm two women down, and I'm up for the task. "That's great, Stella." I step onto the tile floor, relieved Stella was able to clean it all up because Abby's tone led me to believe I was going to need my wet vac. "No water damage, so that's a positive sign."

"Thank God. Mom is already so stressed, and I thought maybe I broke it by overstuffing it. I was only trying to help, though. She's been too busy to get to the laundry."

I get down on my haunches and spot the problem right away, there's a small leak right under the circular window of the front-load washing machine. "Oh, you didn't break it. These things happen."

The washer is about ten years old, but still in great condition. I open the door, and point to the washer door boot gasket. "See this thing here. It just needs replacing. They get worn out and rip which is where the water came from. It's an easy fix if that's all it is. Low-key problem," I say with confidence, although I could be using the term wrong.

Stella pulls her phone from her sweatshirt pocket. Of course she's not interested in a washing machine repair lesson. "Cool," she says, her face lowering to her screen. She's relieved, I'm sure, but has clearly moved on now that she knows this is a pretty minor deal.

Our heads turn when we hear the front door slam. "Oh my fucking God, Stella, is the entire house flooded? I got home as soon as I could. Ouch!"

Stella runs from the laundry room, "It's fine, Mom, just a minor problem with the boot thing on the door. Are you okay?"

The rhythmic click of shoes over hardwood gets louder. "Yeah, I just tripped over that damn tool box thing by the front door." Abby's long strides stop abruptly when she grabs the door frame, sending her long blond waves over her shoulders. Her crystal blue eyes meet mine, and the color of her full lips match her flushed cheeks.

Abby is like a storm that came out of nowhere, stopping herself right before she rips through me.

A wave of coconut scent floats through the air, and I quickly scan her curvy hips. The shape of her thighs are visible thanks to her black leggings and I remember I'm at a client's house, not here to rescue a single mom by fixing all her problems, taking her out for dinner, then peeling those leggings off her body. "I'm sorry ... that was my ... tool bag." Shaking my head, I try to pull myself out of this very intoxicating state of hypnosis. *Of course it was your tool bag, you idiot.* "It's just a minor problem. I can order the part and fix this for you in a few days. The bad news is you can't do any laundry until I fix it." I clear my throat. "Unless you have the time to stand here and mop up the water."

"Well, I don't." Her voice is gentler than before, but still laced with panic.

I laugh, but Abby doesn't join me. "That was a joke. Obviously you don't have time to mop up water." I feel like such an idiot. The last thing this woman needs is for me to try to shed light on the fact that she's already pushed to the max, spread so thin she can barely think.

Abby's chest heaves and she paces the floor of her small laundry room. I lower my eyes to my covered boots to avoid watching her ass move in those amazing leggings. Stella hasn't come back into the laundry room, but I'm not sure where she is, and I don't want her to catch me checking out her mom. Or have Abby catch me for that matter. I'm a pretty nice-looking guy, but I'm not so arrogant as to think that me checking her out is going to make her day or anything.

It sure makes mine though. Abby is all woman. She's got substance, she's lived a life. I've tried dating a few women my age, and they are all great in their own ways, but they don't hold my attention. Honestly, the times I've attempted to have a relationship with anyone, it feels like I'm trying to satiate my hunger with a zero-calorie snack. Not that I'd ever say that out loud.

"Yeah, I don't have time for anything. I haven't even gotten a tree or started shopping, and obviously I haven't done laundry in a week." Her voice cracks and she crosses her arms over her chest. "I'm sorry, I'm just stressed. And babbling like an asshole. It's been a long day."

"You called the right guy. Once I get the part, I'll get over here and have you up and running in no time," I say knowing as soon as I get that boot gasket, I'll drop everything and be right back in this cramped room, hopefully with Abby looking over my shoulder, as soon as humanly possible. "I was raised by a single mom. I get it."

I've just met this woman and fuck, she's a *woman*. I don't

know a thing about her, except that she's a single mom with flowing blond hair, hypnotizing blue eyes, curves that literally stop my heart, and she came bursting through the door like a storm that has the power to uproot trees.

She's so exasperated and stressed, her labored breathing makes me want to do everything I can to calm her. And the thing that makes me a little nervous is that I know I'll try if she lets me.

CHAPTER 4

Abby

There's something about this young man standing in my laundry room that reassures me. Christ, this is the most calm I've felt all day, and there's no doubt in my mind he'll fix my leak, er, the washer leak. His full head of dark brown hair is shaved close to his perfect head, and he has eyes so dark they're almost black. He turns away from me and I can't help but let my eyes wander over his perky ass and thick thighs. Matthew who? The image of Matthew's stupid head between my legs has officially been replaced.

If I didn't know better, I'd think Dylan was checking me out—actually no! I'm not falling for that bullshit again. I bet all the fuckboys in town have a running bet to see who can be the fastest to pick up forty-something single moms. Like it's a secret club and they think they are doing women like me some kind of favor via fake flattery. No, thank you. I still regret throwing away that chocolate cake. Never again.

I'm even surprised at how fast I can romanticize a man without even knowing him. I squint. "What's your name again?"

He clears his throat. "It's Dylan. And you're Abby. My aunt told me. I'm good with names."

His voice is deep, and I pictured a much older man when we spoke on the phone. "And how long have you been doing this?" I ask, because I realize I'm completely trusting a stranger to come into my house and fix something that I need to use every single day. Well, who am I kidding? I don't do laundry every single day but I use my machine at least once a week. I think.

Or maybe I do trust him, but I don't trust myself because I'm just trying to keep him here longer. Dammit, there's not enough chocolate cake in this world that can cure my craving for scruff like his on my neck, between my thighs, rubbing against my—

"Nine years." Dylan puffs out his chest and his cheeks swell above his five o'clock shadow.

"Nine years?" I ask.

He nods. "Nine years. Started the day after I graduated high school."

Okay, so that makes him about twenty-seven? I wring my hands together, and double check the math in my head. "Hmm, nine years."

"Oh, my God, Mom. Nine years, okay?" Stella yells from the living room. Everything I do these days annoys her, and her comments are white noise to me at this point. I'm sure as soon as Dylan leaves she's going to tell me I was low-key annoying her the entire time he was here.

"That's just ... a really young age to start a business."

"Yeah," Dylan lowers his head. "My mom, she got sick, and I wanted to, had to, do something to try to help. Made me grow up damn fast, that's for sure."

I nod as the puzzle pieces click together in my mind. It makes sense that Dylan went through something to make him grow up fast because I sense he's a lot older than he says. It has nothing to do with his looks. It's in the way he carries himself, how calm I feel around him. Which scares the shit out of me for some reason.

"Oh, I'm sorry about that."

"I appreciate that, Abby." Dylan smiles wider, making my heart pump a little too fast which tells me my interrogation shouldn't be over yet. Sure, I'm aroused by the way his pushed-up sweater sleeves expose the muscles and tendons of his forearms, but what happened to me on Saturday night makes me feel feisty. Like if a young man like this is going to turn me on, I need to take back some control.

"And can you show me exactly what's wrong with the washer?" I tilt my chin up, acting like I'd know what the problem was if he pointed it out. The truth is, I have no freaking idea about any of this shit. He could tell me that this thing was beyond repair or that it would be two thousand dollars to fix, and I wouldn't know the difference. I just hope Stella doesn't come in here and blow my cover. Or rat me out from the living room where she's sitting under a blanket with her face in her phone.

Dylan gets down on his haunches and opens the door. His large hands run along some rubber circle inside the door and his eyes hold mine. "Right there, here, come feel this."

I kneel beside him, feeling his warm breath on my neck. He smells like snow, and he takes my hand and leads it along the rubber thing. His fingers are over mine, leading them along the inside of the rubber opening. I feel a hole, and he pushes our fingers in together. "Oh," I say so loud I startle myself. This reassurance was definitely a good idea. I think.

"You feel that? That's a big hole."

"Yeah, I feel it. You shoved my fingers right in it." He laughs, and I feel the vibration run down my neck. My shoulders rise as if they will protect me from wanting to put my head on his shoulder and inhale his fresh scent.

"That's where all the water is leaking from." His voice is softer than before.

My eyes lock with his. "The water is leaking from the hole." I force down a dry swallow. "Then onto the floor?" *Shut the fuck up, Abby. That's what he just told you. Stop trying to oversee something you know nothing about, set your woman wood aside, and let the man do his job.*

I really should stop fondling his fingers in my washing machine before water comes out of my hole. Standing, I take a step backward, and my face heats. This conversation, one he probably has with housewives around the state, is actually turning me on. Water coming out of the hole and all. There's literally no hope for me. "Well then, it sounds like you know what you're doing."

Dylan slowly rises, his eyes quickly running over my entire body as he does. Or maybe I'm just imagining it, wishing for it.

This guy is closer to my daughter's age than he is to mine, and I know there's nothing intriguing for him to see here. I'm a curvy, older woman, with a teenage daughter, a cluttered house, and clearly in desperate need of his services so I look ridiculous questioning him. Not to mention not having regular sex has me strutting around thinking every man who looks at me twice is a possibility because Lord knows my washing machine isn't the only thing that needs servicing right now.

During my marriage, I put so many things before sex: food, sleep, watching Instagram reels on how to perfect the Boutique Bob. Never again. If I'm ever in a relationship again, my pussy will be open for business at all times. And not just because Ben cheated, but because like Marge said, it really is an important part of a relationship.

"I *do* know what I'm doing, Abby." His voice is low, almost a whisper. And I hope his tone is due to the fact that he's thinking inappropriate thoughts too. "I've been fixing things around my house since I was a kid. My dad was never around and Mom and I ... well, we figured a lot of stuff out."

Dylan is such a *man*. Like a real man who knows how to fix things and take charge and calm me down. I try to ignore the goosebumps that sprout all over my body, but it's no use. I had my fingers in a hole in my washing machine with this man, big deal. I'm sure this is just a regular service call for him. I must smell like desperation and hair spray.

Dylan retrieves his phone from his back pocket. "I should have the part in a few days. Three at the most. Since my aunt called from her phone, I need your number so I can schedule the repair when it comes in."

After giving him my number, I say, "Well, thank you. I really do appreciate you coming out here so fast." I'm an asshole, the man got here in less than an hour, and in the half hour I've spent with him, all I can do is drill him with questions about doing his job, all the while I want his hands in something else besides my washer. I'm secretly accusing him of mocking me after what happened at Ivory's wedding. Could I be any more self-involved? I'm low-key messed up, as Stella would say.

When Dylan clears his throat and takes a step closer to me, my stomach comes alive with a million butterfly wings.

It's then that I realize I'm blocking the doorway, and he'd probably like to leave.

"Oh, sorry, "I say, spinning on my boot heel. "It's been a long day. I said that already, I think."

Dylan puts his hand on my shoulder as we head into the living room. "Well, hopefully I put your mind at ease."

I need to stop being the helpless, horny housewife. It really doesn't suit me. "You did, thanks," I answer, and he drops his hand just as we spot Stella, her cell phone three inches from her face.

"What's for dinner, Mom? I'm starving. And please don't say pasta again."

I was totally going to make pasta again. A scratch dinner isn't going to happen tonight. Or probably anytime before the year is over. My feet are throbbing, and as soon as this young man leaves, I'm peeling off these boots and getting out of the Spanx and legging torture device I poured myself into this morning.

Guilt pools in my belly, we have had pasta so much lately I'm not even sure I can stomach it.

"Maybe we can order pizza from Patty's Place?" I offer.

Stella shoots up as Dylan picks up his toolbox. "Oh, then can we please, please, get a tree? There's less than two weeks left, Mom."

I'm so tired that the thought of getting a tree and putting it up makes me want to vomit. But I love Stella so much and I don't want her to think, for one minute, that getting a tree and enjoying the holidays with her is too much for me. Because it's not. She's my world. I just wish there was more of me to go around. I never thought being a single mom would be easy, but I had no idea it'd be this hard. If I didn't have such supportive parents, I don't know where Stella and I would be right now.

More guilt consumes me, and I try to blink back tears. "Tomorrow night, honey, I promise." I take a deep breath. *You can do this. You can handle it all. It will be okay.*

Dylan's hand is on the handle and he sends me a sympathetic smile before opening the door. "Okay, I'll see you soon. Enjoy that pizza, kiddo." He waves before heading out the door.

I saunter to the sofa and sit next to Stella. Her thumbs are sliding over the screen, typing feverishly. "What kind of pizza, my love?"

"Just cheese. And you promise we can get a tree tomorrow?"

"I promise, honey." I wrap my arm around her shoulders and pull her close. "I'm sorry I've been such a mess lately. I'm going to do better."

Stella drops her phone and I run my fingers through her loose ponytail. She rests her head on my chest. "You aren't a mess Mom, you're doing a great job."

When she wraps her arms around my waist, a few tears fall from my eyes. I hate getting so stressed out about trivial stuff. I have my health; I have my beautiful daughter; I have a job I love; I have a home I adore. And I'm thankful for it all. Everything I need is right here.

"Oh, Mom?"

"Yes, my love?"

"That guy was totally into you. He's cute. You should date him."

A laugh erupts out of me. Hearing my daughter tell me some young guy has the hots for me, as much as I want to believe it, is literally hysterical. I'm sure she could tell I was the one who was desperately into him for the little time he was here, and this is a pity-compliment.

I kiss the top of Stella's head before getting up to get my phone from my purse so I can order the pizza, then peel off my layers and breathe normally.

A text from an unknown number lights up my screen: *Hey, it's Dylan. I just remembered I'm going to have to come and check on one more thing as soon as I can. Does tomorrow night work? Want to make sure you're home.*

CHAPTER 5
Dylan

Just text her now. Before you lose the nerve. My palms sweat as I stop at the end of Abby's dead-end street and tap on her number.

Maybe surprising her with a Christmas tree tomorrow night is crossing a line, but I'll always remember what my mom said one night while playing cards with her friend, Joan. "I'd only let a man into our life if he made it easier," she'd whispered. Then the two of them laughed about how men like that were extinct. From that day on, I wanted to make her life easier. And I know I did. It wasn't hard either. If she was low on energy, I'd make dinner and clean up. If the lawn needed mowing, I'd do it. If her car sounded funny, I'd call Joan's husband and let him know.

I'm not an experienced dater, and I've done a little sleeping around, as much as I hate to admit it. But those women were my age or younger, and they didn't scratch my itch. I need depth, someone who has experienced some hardships because I certainly have. There's something about Abby that makes me want to be of service to her. In more ways than one. Like it feels completely natural to me to help her, and I don't think I could stop myself if I tried. I've never experienced this longing before, and it makes sense. All this time, I've needed an older woman to satiate me.

Tomorrow night I'll know if bringing her a Christmas tree is too much. For now, all I can think about is surprising her, so making her think I need to go over there again in order to fix her washing machine seems justified. Telling her I'll be dropping off a tree doesn't.

I shoot off the text and wait a good five minutes at the end of her road. Nothing.

Abby is a busy, single mom. I can be patient. I could tell by the way she got all misty, how her face dropped when Stella asked her about getting a tree, that she was overwhelmed. And damn if I didn't want to relieve her of some of her burdens right then and there. Instead, I picked up my tools and racked my brain, thinking of something I could do for her.

Before pulling onto the main road, I look up the number to Noah's Hardware. He has the best trees in town, and when I drove by this morning, I saw he was restocked. There's a good chance he may be sold out already—people travel from up to fifty miles away to Leeds Falls to get one of his beauties —but if it's meant to be, he'll have a nice tree that I can bring to Abby and Stella tomorrow.

"Hey, Noah, it's Dylan from Applied Appliance."

"My man!" he shouts so loud I laugh. "What can I do for ya?"

"Well, I have an emergency. Got any trees left?"

"For you? Of course. But what happened to the one you got three weeks ago? Don't tell me that fucker dried out."

I shake my head. "No, brother, my tree is amazing. I love it. This one is for someone else. Hoping you have something on the smaller side, she doesn't have a lot of space."

The sound of the bell over Noah's door comes through the phone. "Let me see what I've got for one of my best customers." I spend almost as much money at Noah's as I do at my suppliers. So many people need their appliances fixed right away and can't always wait for parts to be delivered, especially this time of year. There's nothing as heartbreaking as getting a call from someone who's hosting a holiday dinner or party and their oven shits the bed the night before. Noah has saved my ass more than once, that's for sure.

I hold my breath as wind and rustling comes through the phone.

"You're in luck! All my big trees are gone, but Rosemary always makes sure we have some skinnier, smaller trees because those are her favorite. I've got two left. I'll throw a "sold" tag on the best one?"

I blow out a breath and slam my palm on the steering wheel. "Yes! I'll pick it up tomorrow afternoon. Thanks, man!"

Snowflakes fall making the roads slick and wet. I've got a busy day tomorrow, but I'll make the time to deliver that tree. Obviously, Abby doesn't have to be home. I could just leave it on her front steps, I guess. But I want her to see it before she goes out and spends time and money looking for one. That way, she and Stella can have a night in and decorate, or just relax and enjoy the balsam scent.

I pull in my driveway, cut the engine to my truck, and check my phone before going inside. My heart swells when I see Abby responded to my text: *Stella has a basketball game after school, then we'll be home around five. Can you make it quick? Going to get a tree.*

Sure can, I type back, debating whether to tell her I have something that will make her life a little easier because I don't want the conversation to end. I want to ask her if she's feeling better, what kind of pizza they got, if she's ever considered dating a younger man.

"Slow down," I say out loud as if it will keep me from

thinking about her silky hair and the way her hips curve below her narrow waist. "Slow down. What makes you think that woman has any use for you?"

Just as I'm about to slide my phone back into my pocket and head inside, Aunt Marge lights up my screen. *How'd the service call go, dear? Were you able to help? And I know I mentioned this, but she's single. Just in case you forgot.*

CHAPTER 6

Abby

As soon as Stella's game ends and she runs to the locker room with her team, I pull my phone from my purse. My foot taps at turbo speed as I open my text thread with Dylan. I've read it ten times today, what's once more?

After confirming a time, I asked Dylan what his extra trip was about. He responded with: *Let's just say it will make your life easier, I promise.*

I cringe at my response, wishing I could take it back. Did I really need to say, *Oh, a man who keeps his promises? How novel.*

I really wanted to respond with, *I'll tell you something that could make my life easier.* Of course I didn't. Last night I had gone from accusing Dylan of fake-checking me out, to questioning his profession, to lusting after him in under a half hour. I let my Bitter Divorced Woman show, too. My sister, Rebecca is right, my emotions are always all over my face and it's really something I should learn how to control. Especially at my age. I've given up on having a close relationship with my sister. Maybe I should give up on relationships altogether and save myself.

I think you haven't been hanging out with the right men. Or man I should say, had been Dylan's response. I've been thinking about it all day. Of course I stopped texting him after that. How inappropriate for me to be flirting with a man who's eighteen years younger than me and is probably just doing his due diligence, trying to make an older woman's day.

Last night I couldn't sleep. Sometime around midnight while I was all twisted up in my sheets, trying to erase the way his fingers felt over mine, I sent a screenshot of my conversation with Dylan to Ivory and Lila along with a brief description of what happened. Okay, it probably wasn't that brief, but there was a lot to say about my interlude with the young appliance repairman.

I wasn't expecting Ivory to respond so quickly, or even at all, since she's on her honeymoon, but she came through with: *Pounce on that man. He's worth a test drive, right?*

Lila was more rational: *Ivory's been into the Moscato again, I think. Get to know him a little more, then pounce only if he's good enough for you, Abby. Remember, we do the choosing here!*

My friends keep me grounded, and I know that's a tough job. They never shame me for practically draping myself in every red flag a man shows. Remind me I deserve more than I'm settling for? Yes. But shame me? Never. I can't seem to help it though. I'm a magnet for unworthy men. I'm like a cobra and they're playing one of those hypnotic musical instruments.

Either Dylan really is a good guy who's flirting with me, or I'm imagining it, but he knows how to get me to drop trou faster than I can down a large fry order alone in my car. I'm going to put my money on the latter.

. . .

I pull in the driveway twenty minutes after five. Dylan's truck is parked on the street and adrenaline spiders through my body. Stella notices there's a tree thrown in the truck bed before I do and she jerks toward me. "Oh yeah! We're getting a tree tonight! You promised!"

I slowly nod. "Yes, we will, honey. Dylan just needs to take another look at the washing machine, so while he's doing that, I'll throw some sandwiches together and we can eat on the way. You must be starving after playing so hard tonight."

"Yeah, not hard enough though. We freaking lost again."

I cut the engine and turn toward my daughter. "You did great, honey. And you're a *team*. It's not all on you."

She shrugs, then says, "I know," before opening the car door and sprinting into the house. Of course she didn't bring her coat. I watch her scurry over the snow-covered yard and shake my head. I know she's let down about the game, but I've always loved how resilient Stella is. She has a way of letting go, an art I know nothing about, and she certainly isn't an overthinker like I am.

Before I get out of the car, I take a quick look in the rearview mirror, and my mouth goes dry.

I had made sure to freshen my makeup before I left work, and had on my favorite jeans. I had told myself that taking a little extra care in my appearance today had nothing to do with seeing Dylan again, or with his flirty texts, but it had everything to do with it. If it wasn't for his drop-in, I'd be in sweats and certainly wouldn't have asked Grace to style my hair in the only ten-minute gap between clients that I'd had.

"You're late," Dylan says, the silhouette of his tall frame opening his tailgate. "You told me you only had a minute, but I hope you can give me at least five." He leans over and wraps a very large, sexy hand around the tree trunk and pulls it from his truck. I bite my bottom lip.

Standing the tree on the ground, his eyes find mine, a pleased smile plastered on his ridiculously handsome face.

I'm walking toward him so fast it's practically a jog. "I'm always late. Sorry about that. And I guess I can give you five minutes, but what's with the tree? I thought you were coming to look at my washer again."

"Hmm, did I say that? That I was coming to look at your washing machine again? I don't recall saying that." He squints his dark eyes like he's deep in thought, and I sneak a look at the sliver of skin that shows just above his belt as he grips the tree.

Suddenly, I'm not cold. In fact, there's an inferno burning in my chest and down to my love canal, as I think about where Dylan's happy trail leads.

I need to pull myself together, get laid, or do a face-plant in the snow.

"Well, I just assumed that's what you wanted. Listen, that's a very nice tree you have there. I can tell you're really excited about it. But it's freezing out here, and I promised my daughter we'd get our tree tonight. I'm just about to crumble into a pile, I'm so tired and—"

"Easy there, Stormy," Dylan interrupts, throwing the tree over his shoulder, exposing the V-shaped muscle of his obliques.

I'm not a religious woman, but the good Lord needs to have mercy on my soul right now. Or Dylan's, if he doesn't get away from me with that tree balancing on his broad shoulder, showing off how well he can handle heavy things.

"Stormy?" I question, trying to focus on his dark eyes and scruff that surrounds his full lips instead of his trail of happiness.

"Yeah, Stormy. You came into your house last night like a storm, and when you got out of your car just now, you made it to me so fast I felt a breeze."

I cross my arms. "I don't know if I like that nickname."

He raises his eyebrows. "I won't use it anymore then, but I feel the need to tell you I want to calm that storm inside of you."

My stomach contracts, and there's a gush between my legs. Okay, now I fucking love that nickname. Dylan can call me whatever he wants, and I need to do everything in my power to hide the fact that I'm lusting after this man who's young enough to be my son. "Oh, in that case maybe it's not so bad." I shrug.

"Well, I'll only call you Stormy when it's absolutely necessary. How's that?" Dylan heads to my front door, his work boots crunching in the thin layer of snow.

I clear my throat. "That's acceptable, I guess. But what are you doing, Dylan?"

He turns to face me, and I swear the misty cloud that leaks out of his mouth when he blows out a long breath is the shape of a penis. Damn, I hope my vibrator is charged. "Abby, this tree is for you and Stella. I wanted to do something for you. Something nice. Like I said, I grew up with a single mom, and well, seeing you the other night ... you seemed so done, so depleted. I hated it and I wanted to do something for you. That's what I mean when I tell you I want to calm that storm raging inside you."

I swallow hard, the tears already forming. No man has ever really seen me. Not like this. Not even Ben knew how bad I was struggling, trying to balance work and motherhood, or how his affair affected me. And it wasn't because I didn't let him know how I felt. I was crystal clear about that. It was because he didn't *want* to see me. He refused because it was too hard for him, and he couldn't handle it.

It's all so touching, but I'm silly to think this young man is interested in me. Dylan feels *sorry* for me, and fuck me, but I remind him of his *mother* of all people. I'm sure she's a lovely woman, but his mother? Not quite the vibe I was getting from him but what do I know? It's not as if my track record of reading men has been good, why would I trust it now?

"Well, that's nice, thank you. I appreciate you taking pity on a divorced woman who's old enough to be your mom."

Dylan slides the tree off his shoulder and carefully stands it on the ground. "That's not what this is." He shakes his head and laughs.

"I'm glad this is so amusing to you. That I can be your entertainment for the night, and you compare my lifestyle, the one I'm desperately trying to hold together with what feels like very weak hands, to a storm, a freaking storm."

His smile falls into a straight line. The man looks like I just punched him in the gut, and a wave of satisfaction runs through me. "Like I said, Abby, a storm I want to calm. I want to help. Not because I pity you, or because you remind me of my mom. It's because this is what feels right to me, natural. But mostly because I'm attracted to you. You have substance, you're an amazing mom. And have you seen your ass? You're stunningly beautiful in every way."

His eyes run down my body, and I brace myself for his punch line. This has to be another dude trying to win a bet with his friends.

The raw night air hits me, and I shiver. If Dylan is being serious, he really would calm the storm blowing around inside me, the one that never lets me rest because I'm so afraid that if I do, everything will go to shit. God, he's good. Too good to be true that is.

"I'm almost twenty years older than you. You're being silly."

He takes another step closer, and the tree falls to the glittery ground. "You see numbers. I see an opportunity. Maybe I am being silly. But regardless, I wanted to come here tonight to do this for you and to see you. I am younger, but I'm more mature than most men my age, I can guarantee you that. I see who you are, and if you let me take you on a date, you'll see the age difference doesn't matter at all."

I can't even begin to argue with him because his words are music to my ears. My body moves toward him, our eyes locked. "You want to calm my storm, do you? Hmm, well, I'm always late. For everything, all the time. I have a teenage daughter and well, we get our period at the same time and it's a fucking treat. I work fifty hours a week to make ends meet, and my ex-husband cheated on me so I'll probably never trust you. Oh, and I'm thick if you didn't notice, which I'm pretty sure you did. I've always been a bigger woman, and I always will be. If you think I'm giving up chocolate cake, pizza, or french fries to be one of those tiny gym girls, think again. I like my Charmin Layer, okay?!" I'm practically yelling at him, talking so fast I sound like a disclaimer at the end of a pharmaceutical ad.

I'm breathless as Dylan closes the gap between us and says. "That makes two of us then." His eyes fall to half moons. "You got anything else?"

"No." I take a step back so his testosterone is away from my nostrils because I'm growing more feral by the second.

"Well, if that's all you got, can I just say, if you're trying to scare me away it's not working, Stormy."

He runs his hand through my hair and I barely squeak out, "I thought you weren't going to call me that unless it was absolutely necessary." *Please call me that again. Please calm my storm. Please don't be fucking around with me.*

"That's right." His voice is slow and deep as he drops his hand, then bends down and lifts the tree over his shoulder again. "You going to show me where you want this tree, or would you like me to go?"

CHAPTER 7
Dylan

"I guess it's okay if you stay. Maybe you can help me get it up?"

"Hmm, isn't that my line?" I ask just before Abby opens her front door. Maybe the joke is a tad early, but I have a feeling Abby needs a tension release.

A smile plays on her lips and she sucks in her cheeks, obviously trying to hide the fact that she finds my joke funny. Which makes me happy, but I want her to see so much more. I make my way into her living room, slide the tree off my shoulder, and lean it against the wall by the front door.

"Okay, no more bad jokes. I promise," I respond as Stella comes barreling down the stairs. I don't want Abby to think I'm completely oblivious, and that I don't know how to act around kids. "Where would you like this? Need me to move any furniture?"

"Oh, is that our tree? It's so pretty! Mom, I didn't know you were going to surprise me! And Dylan, I didn't know you delivered trees!" Stella throws her phone on the couch and runs her hand over the branches.

"I only deliver for special customers," I answer, winking at

Abby. I cross my arms over my pride-swollen chest. While I was hoping to take some of Abby's load off her shoulders, I didn't consider how happy it would make her daughter.

Stella's eyes move between Abby and me. "I told you he liked you, Mom."

Abby gasps then says, "Stella!" Her face turns crimson and the color travels down her neck.

Stella laughs as she reaches for her phone and starts typing away.

"What?" I ask, raising my hands in the air. "She's right, Abby. I do like you." My gaze is fixed on Abby, and when she finally looks at me, I quickly run my eyes down the length of her. Her hips look amazing in her jeans, and she's wearing more makeup than she was last night. God, she's a natural beauty, a woman who can roll out of a bed in a T-shirt and look just as stunning as she does right now with perfect waves in her hair and glossy lips. I mean, I haven't seen it yet, but I can tell. Of course I can't wait to see how right I am. I just need Stormy to let me take her out on a proper date first. One thing at a time, of course.

Hopefully, I'll have a chance to ask her tonight because there's no way I can wait any longer. But I don't want to interrupt her night with her daughter. Mom and I would always have so much fun stringing popcorn and making paper chains after going out in the woods behind our house to find the perfect tree.

So if I ask Abby out and she tells me she's not interested or not in a place to date, I'll leave her alone. It will be hard as hell, but I'll do it. For now, I'm here to help her, and show her I want to get to know her if she'll have me.

After setting up the tree in the corner to the right of her gas fireplace, Stella's phone buzzes, and she races for the stairs. Taking two steps at a time, she hollers, "I'll be back down to decorate, but it's Lauren!"

As soon as Stella is out of sight, Abby says, "Lauren is her best friend. Those two are inseparable."

Abby plops on the sofa and stares at the tree, a look of wonderment in her eyes. "This was so nice of you, Dylan."

My heart rate picks up, and I take advantage of our time alone. Then, I'll let her have some special time with Stella. "Your daughter is right. I do like you. And I want to take you out. Tomorrow night."

She rubs the back of her neck and shifts in her seat.

When she doesn't answer, I continue, "You and Stella were talking about how she'd be with her dad tomorrow while I was putting up the tree."

Abby leans forward and rests her elbows on her knees as I sit beside her, my heart pounding under my chest so loud she can probably hear it.

"Is this a joke, Dylan? What does a young guy like you want with a forty-five-year-old single mom?" She looks around her messy living room and points to a few empty water bottles sitting on her black coffee table. "Who's clearly a scattered mess."

I want to wrap my arms around her shoulders and hold her, the need to touch her feels as natural as breathing. Can you really explain things like chemistry and feeling an instant connection with someone? Especially when you've never felt it so strong? "I can assure it's not a joke. And have you seen yourself? You're a complete knockout. You're funny. And I love how real you are. I love that you're older. You've been through a lot, like me. I think we are more alike than you realize."

Her jaw slacks, and I swear to God if we were the only ones in this house right now, I'd kiss this woman. Slow and deep, then fast and hard.

Abby playfully slaps me on the arm, and her cheeks get pink again. "Why not go for women your age? Do you have a fetish or something? Is it a competition with your friends to see how many older women you can pound?"

I raise my eyebrows and chuckle. "Pound? Well, I wasn't expecting that to come out of your mouth."

"I say what I want when I want I guess. I am a middle-aged woman, not a nun."

"Fair enough. But again, you're wrong. Women my age are fine and all, they've just never done much for me. I've tried, but I get bored. My mom always told me I was an old soul. I've always had older friends, and liked to talk with the adults when I was younger. And you ... well, I'm drawn to your energy. The way you burst through the door last night, then started questioning me. I instantly felt calm and relaxed. Like I was home, even though you were interrogating me. I know it probably doesn't make sense."

We both laugh. "I don't want to be taken advantage of. I have to ask questions."

My smile drops. "Of course you do. Ask away, please. Then I'm going to leave so you and Stella can enjoy your night. Quality time alone with your child when you are a single parent is tough to come by, I'm sure. There's always so much to do. Mom told me over and over how sacred her life with me was, and she didn't want anyone to disrupt our traditions."

"I appreciate that, Dylan. Thank you." Abby bites her bottom lip before asking, "Okay, then I have another question for you. If I was to say yes to your ... offer, where would you take me tomorrow night?"

CHAPTER 8
Abby

The legs of my velvet pants swish as I pace my bedroom floor. "Just send me a picture of your outfit. I'm sure you look great," Lila says, clearly out of breath.

I stop dead in my tracks when I hear a grunt come through the phone. "Did I just hear Holt ... growl?" If I'd known she was in the middle of something, I wouldn't have called her. I mean, I'm going to go out with Dylan regardless, but I guess letting my friends know about the age difference makes me feel more responsible. Every woman needs validation sometimes, and I'm no different. Especially since my entrance back into the dating scene has been so rocky. Okay, who am I kidding? It's been a serious shitshow.

Lila giggles. "I'm sure you look amazing, you always do. And just go have fun. Who cares about his age? Holt!"

Rustling is followed by Holt's deep voice. "Abby, stop worrying and enjoy yourself. From what I've heard you yammer about in the last ten minutes, he's more of a man than those other guys you've taken for a test drive. By far. He doesn't care about what you're wearing either. Now I have to tend to my woman before she falls asleep on the sofa in front of this Hallmark movie. Text us after your date."

The line goes dead, and I stare at my phone in disbelief. If Holt thinks he's going to turn our threesome into a foursome, he's got another thing coming. Although I do trust him, he's a wonderful man, and he's absolutely right—Dylan is way more of a man than any guy I've dated. Or gone out with. Or ever talked to in my entire life. Fine, I guess he can join our club.

I pull at the waist of my wide leg pants and stand on my toes. Maybe a little heel will make me feel better? As I head to my closet, I hear a knock at the door. Either Dylan is early, or I did a terrible job of estimating just how long it would take me to get ready for this date. We're just going to the local movie theater to see *It's A Wonderful Life*. This time of year, they always play Christmas classics and have a full dinner menu. It's already dark outside, and it will be dark in the theater, but I want to look good. Like really good. Twenty years younger good.

My pulse quickens as I head downstairs, the nerves I've pushed away all day are front and center. When I open my front door, Dylan greets me with a rubber ring adorned with a bow. I'm not sure if it's a joke, or something he made for me out of recycled materials to hang on my door. "Um, that's pretty!"

"Pretty? Ha! It's your part. It came in early! I can put this in before the movie if I'm quick."

Yeah, you can put my part in as quickly as you want, you sexy repairman, you. "Oh! That's great. Are you sure?" I'm so glad I'm not going to have to hang up what I thought was a God awful decoration, but I'm even happier I can start doing laundry again.

He hands me the gasket and bends over to untie his black leather boots, sending a scent of cloves through my nostrils. Dylan's black sweater hugs his thick arms, and his hair and beard are freshly trimmed. When he straightens, his dark eyes smile.

"I'm sure, Abby," he says as he takes long strides to my laundry room. His black jeans cup his ass so well, and I wonder what he has on under there. Boxer briefs? Oh, maybe black ones. Tight black ones. I squeeze the rubber ring so hard, I check for puncture wounds as we cram into the tiny space.

Dylan faces me. "I haven't told you how sexy you look tonight, have I?" His eyes travel over me and he pulls at my white fitted sweater. "I like this. You look great in white."

I clear my throat. "Thanks. You look … great too." Dylan looks so great, in fact, that I'd like him to slide off that belt. Hearing it hit the tile floor would be music to my ears as he wraps his strong arms around me. What can I say? Since my divorce, I've turned into a romantic with a nasty mind. I want him now. And trying to tame these urges is getting harder by the second.

Dylan doesn't drop his gaze and I flush, feeling like he can read my mind. When he holds out his hand, my eyes go wide. Okay, I guess we're getting this party started.

"I, um, need that." He points to the rubber ring.

I hand it to him then take a step back. "Oh, yes, of course you need that. My … I mean the part. You need it to fix the washer. Here, let me give you some space." I take a few steps backward and run into the doorjamb.

Thankfully, Dylan doesn't notice because he's already on his knees peering into my washer. "I just need to pull out your old one then get this one in. Sometimes you have to wrestle with these, but I'm sure it won't take me long to slide it in."

It won't take me long to slide it in. My vagina has a heartbeat. Why does everything he says sound like dirty talk? Either I'm long overdue for a good fucking, or Dylan is trying to prime me for later. I lean against the door frame since my legs aren't able to support me, as I think about Dylan and me wrestling before he slides it in.

When he reaches over his head and pulls his sweater off, revealing a fitted black tank top, my jaw drops. Dylan's shoulders are made up of peaks and valleys I didn't know existed on the human body, and you can see his back muscles ripple through the fabric. His thick arms are so defined, I want to reach over and see if they are real. I'll probably need my tongue for that, of course.

He grunts as he gets the gasket in place, and a map of veins make their way down his biceps and forearms. If we never make it to the movie tonight, I'll be satisfied with this viewing. There's a part of me that wonders if I should really be standing in the doorway, watching this man pull and stretch the rubber ring to fit my washing machine, but my legs couldn't move right now even if my smoke alarms went off.

After a solid half hour, Dylan stands and wipes the sweat from his brow with the back of his hand. "You're good to go, Stormy."

Ah, that name again. Why does it turn me on so much? Is it because Dylan said he wants to calm that part of me? Or maybe it's the fact that he is standing so close, staring me down with dark eyes. And a pair of arms that could easily toss me around.

"Thank you so much. You're a lifesaver."

He lifts his tank top to wipe his forehead and my lady bits go hot. No more velvet pants around Dylan, my poor pussy is overheating.

When I open my mouth to ask him how much I owe him, he takes a step toward me and says, "Don't worry about it. Merry Christmas. It's my gift to you."

"But you already gave me a tree. And I want to pay you. You came over and took care of me—I mean *it*—so quickly."

He shakes his head and pulls at the hem of my sweater as I

crash into him. "I like you, Abby. I wanted to take care of this for you. Let me."

I'm instantly wet, and it's not from my hot bloomers either. Dylan knows how to take charge in all the right ways, and right now, I'd let Dylan do anything he wants.

Before I know it, I'm voicing my thoughts out loud. "Okay, I'll let you. You know how to take charge, don't you?"

He nods. "I do. I had to start doing it at a young age and honestly? I've always liked it. Helping people gives me a purpose."

Dylan presses his hips against mine, pinning me to the wall with his body. "Do you have anything else around here that needs fixing?"

Sweet Baby Jesus, am I in heaven? I arch my back and my chest heaves. Dylan is good. Too good. Like he's studied romance novels and oh, I don't know, lived in my head so he knows that boning a hot blue-collar man who comes to my house to fix shit is my favorite fantasy.

Something is telling me Dylan doesn't do this with all the housewives in Leeds Falls, but I could be wrong. And right now, I don't care. I'll worry about that later. At this moment, no one can peel me away from Dylan's services.

Wrapping my arms around his neck, I press my lips to his. I open my mouth for him, the feeling of his tongue exploring my mouth pulls a moan from my throat. When Dylan pulls away and says, "I want to kiss you everywhere, but if I do that, we'll miss the movie." All I can do is nod.

CHAPTER 9
Dylan

"That's ... fine if we miss it," Abby says, her voice cracking. And that's all I need to hear to proceed. I've fixed Abby's washing machine, and now I want her to fix me. As soon as I saw her in that fitted fuzzy sweater, her almond-shaped blue eyes like sapphires, my urge to touch her was bone-deep.

Abby may think I'm too young for her, and it's my job to show her that our eighteen-year age difference is merely a number that stands for nothing. I can tell by the way her eyes drag over my body, how her lips part when I look at her, that she wants this. Maybe not as much as I do, but she wants this.

And just like I did on the first night we met when I came over to evaluate her broken washer, I want to calm this storm brewing inside her. Show her that I'm more than some young guy who can fix things around her house. But my cock needs some fixing right now too, and the only one who can do that is this voluptuous woman with long flaxen hair who's arching her back against the wall and quivering under my touch.

"Abby," I whisper as my mouth makes my way down her neck. "You think I'm too young for you, don't you?"

"I ... I don't know."

I suck on her earlobe and she shivers. "I *want* you to know. I want you to know that I'm not too young for you. Do you understand?"

She moans and wraps a leg around my hips, grinding against me, her hunger and need matching mine.

I pull back and look at her closed eyes before gently wrapping a hand around her neck. "Is this okay?" I whisper.

"Yes, yes." Her eyes open halfway and she sucks in her bottom lip as I gently apply a little pressure around her delicate neck. "I want to taste you, Abby."

Our lips crash together, her tongue soft and warm as it fills my mouth. With my free hand I tug at her flowy pants and pull them down. My hand is still wrapped around her neck, and I pull away from her lips and press my forehead to hers. Abby's pants are just past her hip bones, revealing black lace panties.

I yank them down further and watch my hand slide into the lace.

She swallows hard then gasps, her hips moving as I part her folds. When she grabs the back of my head and takes my bottom lip between her teeth, my rock hard cock twitches, dying to break free. But I can wait. All I care about right now is giving Abby a glimpse of just how well I can take care of her.

"Dylan," she cries, her voice muffles under my open mouth as my fingers move over her swollen clit. She looks so beautiful, so ready, with my rough hand wrapped around the porcelain skin of her neck.

Sliding a finger into her delicate walls, my thumb circles over her clit. Abby's breath catches and I fall to my knees, then slowly lower my hand from her neck and run it down the front of her body. I've never even so much as hit on a customer before, but there's a first time for everything, right?

Abby runs her hands over my freshly shaven head as I rip down her panties to her knees. When she shoves my face into her glistening pussy, matching my energy, I smile as soon as I taste her. She's so delicate and sweet, yet the way she drives my head between her legs, taking charge, showing me what she wants, is the most erotic thing I've ever experienced. I knew I needed an older woman.

Abby told me she's never been with a much younger man, and while I've had a few short relationships with women a few years older than me, this is a first for me, too. I love how we're experiencing something new together.

I flatten my tongue over her center and move my head from side to side slowly. I want to savor her delicious scent, taste her as long as I can, but Abby moans and clutches my head, guiding me to go faster. Oh, this is a fun game.

Reaching up, I press her hips against the wall. I let her take control here, but I want to take it back and show her I'll please her without her having to do any of the work.

I take her tight little bud into my mouth, sucking and flicking her with my tongue until she trembles and shakes. It's not until she giggles and peels my hands off her hips that I let her free.

Abby's eyes are half-moons as I stand and pull up her pants and panties. She wraps her hands around my neck and tastes her orgasm on my lips, and I pull her close. Our kiss is slow and gentle, so different than it was before. At least fifteen minutes go by before we come up for air.

"I feel like I've been lied to for a really long time." Abby's head is resting on my chest, and we're rocking back and forth in her silent laundry room.

"What do you mean?"

"Well, I've heard from quite a few women that young men don't really ... know what they're doing in the sex department.

That they can't really please a woman the way a more experienced man can. Exactly how experienced are you, Dylan?" Abby pulls away so our eyes meet, her arms thrown over my shoulders.

"Not a ton of experience. I haven't been with a lot of women. But I do pay attention. Like tonight, I paid attention to the way you moved, how your body reacted to me." I tuck a long strand of hair behind her ear.

"And that's another thing." Abby pokes me in the chest. "How is it you seem to know so much about what women need? Most men are completely oblivious and are fine watching a woman run around and take care of everything."

Maybe I do know a lot about women, but it comes with a sad story. I had to pay attention to my mom and how she was feeling every day. It felt like me and her against the world. I never had a strong male role model in my life, but I felt like it was my duty to step up and pay attention, to protect my mom and help her.

I shrug. "Well, I've never met my dad. My mom got sick when I was young, and I knew it was up to me to take care of her, to take care of us."

Abby raises her eyebrows. "Oh, Dylan. I'm so sorry. I can't imagine. I ... Is she still alive?"

"She passed away a few months after I graduated high school. I miss her, but the time we had together, all the things she taught me about how to treat people and get through tough times, have stayed with me."

My heart beats with Abby's as we stand in her laundry room, her face backlit by the little nightlight in the outlet next to the sink. The energy between us shifts, something unspoken exchanged as she pulls me into a hug. "Thank you for sharing that with me, Dylan."

I bury my face in Abby's hair. She thinks I'm in tune with

what she needs, and that makes me really fucking happy. But Abby seems to know exactly what I need, too.

I may be younger than she is by almost twenty years, but I've been around long enough to realize a woman like her is rare. And if she thinks I'm going to let her slip through my fingers because of our age difference, she's wrong.

CHAPTER 10
Abby

"The thing is, we didn't even have sex, and it was, by far, the sexiest experience I've ever had." Goosebumps run up and down my spine as I pull up a chair and plop down. Ivory is back from her honeymoon and she paints a section of Lila's hair then wraps it in foil.

They turn their heads to me. "So what happened?" they demand in unison.

"Out with it already. I'm dying to catch up with you, Abby," Ivory says. The salon is closed after another busy day, and the three of us decided to turn Lila's after-hours hair appointment into a much-needed friend sesh. Ivory showed us all the pictures from her honeymoon, Lila kept hinting about getting married, but wouldn't give us any straight answers, and I was anxiously awaiting my turn.

My toes curl in my leather boots. "He walked into my house wearing all black, holding a rubber ring with a bow on it and said he was going to fix my washer before our date. Which he did. In a tank top. There was grunting and groaning. Then he refused to charge me for it and asked me what else he could do for me. Long story short, he ate my pussy in my laundry room, then we talked until he left at two this morning." The relief I feel after my verbal diarrhea episode is euphoric, and I sit back in my chair and smile. "He's twenty-seven. I know I've mentioned it, but that's eighteen years younger than me."

A brush falls from Ivory's hand. A strange noise floats out of Lila's open mouth, but no words come out.

Waiting the entire evening to tell them about my night with the young, hot, appliance repairman was worth it because as childish as it may be, it feels good to have the top story of the evening.

Ivory bends over to pick up her brush, then straightens and clears her throat. "So the laundry room? How ... like were you—"

"I was against the wall." I rise from my seat and march across the room so Lila and Ivory get a clear view. I lean my back against the wall and arch. "Like this. And he just slid everything down and I'm pretty sure I shoved his head between my legs. I mean, I didn't force feed him. We had the same idea and he was headed there. I just sped things along a little."

I'm flushed thinking of Dylan as I make my way back to my seat.

Lila purses her lips. "You're glowing, Abby! I know you've always been blunt, but the way you talk about him giving you oral sex in your laundry room, like it's a regular occurrence for an appliance repairman to offer that kind of service, cracks me up. When are you going to see him again?"

"Yeah! When?" Lila's hands are folded in her lap, her fingers laced together so tightly her knuckles are white.

"This weekend, while Stella is with Ben. He wants to take me on a proper date. We're going to try to make it to the Rachel Turner opening. But I'll be okay if we don't." I giggle.

Lila points at me. "You better not miss that! You guys have

to go. If Gabe wasn't coming home that night for Christmas break, I'd be there!"

"Yeah, let him take you on a date, Abby. He's obviously crazy about you. The repairs, the tree. My lord. And the laundry room experience sounds a lot like the porn video Rome and I watched on our honeymoon. It's all so romantic ... yet dirty. There's plenty of time after the date to make another fantasy come to life!"

"I'm a big fan of the kitchen myself," Lila says, picking at a fingernail. "But romantic and dirty. That's the best combination."

I love this entire night, this amazing conversation. Women are sexual creatures and we like to talk about it, dammit. How is it that I didn't only find one woman that speaks my language, but two? Our talks like this always flow with no shame or judgment. People walking through the streets of Leeds Falls, peeping in the windows, probably think we're exchanging recipes or discussing the best cellulite-hiding leggings.

I take a deep breath to try to come down from the high I've been floating on all day. Dylan is imprinted in my brain, and the flirty texts we've shared since this morning are the reason for my perma-grin.

"It is. And I'll make sure we go on an actual date. I will. But I know myself. Afterward, I'll want to sleep with him. Like I won't be able to help myself. And you all know what happens after I sleep with a man. I'm hopeless. I don't *fully* ignore red flags, but I'm an expert at, like, diluting them. To pink flags! Those are easier to ignore."

"Listen," Ivory says, grabbing another foil from her stylist station, "We've all been guilty of diluting those red flags after having sex with a man, ignoring certain behaviors because we get attached and crave love and attention."

Lila nods. "Oh, been there. Remember that married man I

had a thing with? I mean, his wife knew, encouraged it even, but still? What was I thinking? I made excuse after excuse to justify it."

"You two have more control than I do, though." I point to Lila. "Like you got yourself out of that married guy thing. Let's be honest, I don't just dilute the red flags to pink, I'll dilute those fuckers until they're white. White fucking flags. Do you see the irony? Isn't a white flag a surrender flag? I literally just ... surrender because I seem to need sex and attention so much that I ignore all the things. Like a man wanting to watch me blow another guy, for fuck's sake!"

The salon is closed, although I'm pretty sure the people stopping to admire the stunning window Lila decorated can hear me.

We're laughing so hard, tears run down our cheeks. I'm glad I'm not alone in this. These women validate me, make me feel human. Divorced friends are priceless.

Lila's hand covers her mouth. "That is perfect. You turn red flags to white. The surrender flag!" Her hand falls, and she cradles her ribs. "I'm sorry, I mean, it's funny, but it's not funny. The shit we've done for a toxic man. But, you live and you learn."

Ivory purses her lips, trying to hold in another fit of laughter.

"Oh, go ahead! Laugh it up, you assholes! I'm so glad my dating life is this entertaining."

"You know we love you, but damn that was funny." Lila wipes a tear away, and her smile falls. "Listen, so far this guy doesn't have any red flags, okay? Trust yourself. He sounds amazing, is doing everything right, and most definitely doesn't need you to tell him how to take care of you this far." She lifts her fountain soda to her mouth, takes a sip, then continues. "Besides, we need to see what's under those jeans of his before we decide if you should continue to see him," she says, like it's a group decision.

Dylan has already lived a full life, that's for sure. After our laundry room interlude, he told me all about his childhood, how much he wanted to be there for his mom, and how dedicated he is to his business. He is sincere, seems honest, and maybe I'm questioning this thing between us because normally, sincere, honest men bore me. They certainly don't soak my undies the way Dylan does. So, can I trust myself? Or are Ben's words about how men don't want a woman my age and size, even though I know how wrong he is, getting to me? Ivory and Lila know what a douchebag Ben is, we've talked about it several times, and wasting more energy on talking about him isn't something I'm going to do tonight. Besides, he said that out of anger because I left him, and he's apologized several times.

But who am I kidding? As much as I'd like to trust myself with a guy who was a newborn while I was unpacking my college dorm room, my ability to ignore the warning sirens when it comes to a hot man is a well-trained muscle. Clearly, I need all the help I can get.

CHAPTER 11

Dylan

"I so appreciate you coming to pick me up." Abby opens the door then fastens a pair of gold hoop earrings in her ears, the plunging neckline of her fitted black dress makes my cock swell.

I step inside and grab her arm before she struts away. There's a pile of clean clothes waiting to be folded on the sofa, and an empty water bottle and stack of papers cover the coffee table. "Where are you running off to, Stormy? Haven't you heard that's what men do? They pick women up, take them on dates, fix things around their house."

Her hands grip my arms as I kiss her pillowy lips. Pulling away, she answers, "Actually, that's all news to me. And I'm sorry. I wasn't running off." She stands on her tiptoes and gives me another kiss then starts to pull away again. I wrap my arms around her, holding her to me. "I'll be right back, I just wanted to throw Stella's basketball uniform in the dryer before we go, and I haven't even done my makeup yet. I got held up at work, then Stella needed a ride to a sleepover because Ben spaced it and couldn't bring her because of a work thing. I'm just ... always running behind, and I wanted to be ready for you. And I'm not."

Abby scrubs her eyebrows then rests her hand back on my biceps. "You take your time. Go get ready, and I'll throw the clothes in the dryer for you. There's no rush, the opening doesn't start for an hour."

Her shoulders relax and her lips curl into a smile. "Thank you. I'm sorry I'm such a scattered mess all the time. You make me feel ... a lot better about it."

"You aren't a mess, you're a single mom. There's a huge difference." I plant a kiss on her forehead, wanting nothing more than to lift the hem of her dress, but there will be time for that later. Abby is excited about going to the opening and I'm determined to ease some of her stress so we can enjoy an incredible evening together.

While she finishes getting ready, I throw the clothes in the dryer, and fill up her tree stand with more water. A few needles fall as I do, so I clean them up, then put the empty water bottle on her coffee table into the recycling bin.

Abby hums along to *White Christmas* as my truck turns onto the main road. Yards and front porches are dusted with the fresh coat of glittery snow that we got this morning, and lights twinkle through windows.

My hand is high on her thigh, the sight of her flushed cheeks and relaxed shoulders makes me happy. I want her to enjoy this date, and the chance to get to know her better has had me buzzing all day. We shared a lot the other night, and it left me wanting more of this woman who makes me laugh, turns me on, and occupies all my thoughts since meeting her.

Abby may think she's a scattered mess, but that's not what I see when I look at her. I see a sexy queen who runs a business, a household, and would do anything for her daughter. Yeah, she turns me the fuck on; I love her full hips and ass, and her narrow waist and luscious thighs are perfection. But there's so much more to her. I know she can do it all herself, but when I'm around, I'll show her she doesn't have to.

"Do you ever look in people's windows? See if you can spot them having dinner or get a peek at how they decorate?" Her voice is soft, and she places her hand over mine.

"I do. Especially this time of year. I love seeing the glow of a Christmas tree through a window. Oh, and there's something about a house with candles in every window. My mom and I would put some on the windowsills every year."

Abby squeezes my hand, and we lock eyes for a second. "Those childhood memories, especially the ones around the holidays are the best, aren't they? I want to create those for Stella. Even though her dad and I divorced, I want her to have great memories. Like I did growing up."

When we pull into the parking lot, the studio is packed. A line forms around the white-washed brick building. The four windows in the front, that are well over six-feet tall, display narrow trees wrapped in twinkle lights. "There's no doubt in my mind that she does, Abby. I know I haven't spent a lot of time with her, but she seems happy. Well adjusted."

Abby smiles, and I cut the engine, then undo my seatbelt. Shifting my entire body so I'm facing her, I ask, "Are you ... do you miss him? Your ex? I know we didn't talk about him much the other night, but you said it's only been a little over a year since you divorced."

Abby shakes her head. "I don't miss him. We drifted, stopped having sex. Then, he had an affair. A customer told me while I was giving her highlights."

Her gaze is fixed straight ahead and a stab of anger runs through me. "Abby, I'm so sorry. A customer told you?"

She laughs. "Can you imagine? And don't be sorry. We weren't in love. It gave me a reason to leave him. I probably would've stayed too, but when I confronted him, he denied it even though I had proof—my customer showed me a screenshot of their texts since he was fucking her best friend—and the scary part was that he lied to me so ... easily. Like it didn't phase him at all to tell me it wasn't true."

So many questions are running through my head. How could someone do that to their family? Why are men such entitled, incompetent creatures? How can I make her see that I'm nothing like her ex-husband?

Instead, I give her space to talk. One thing my mom taught me was when people are telling you deeply personal things about their life, they mostly just want you to listen. Not chime in, not tell them a story about yourself, not give them any advice. Just listen.

"Then, I told him that I had proof, and I was leaving him and you know what he said?"

"That he made the biggest mistake and he'll spend the rest of life making it up to you?"

Abby laughs and her eyes fall to our interlocked fingers. "He said that no man will want me: a chubby, middle-aged woman. It's hard for me to even tell you that. But that was it for me. I didn't have a plan, I didn't know where Stella and I would go. I just knew I had to get out of that relationship."

My nostrils flare, and a wave of heat runs through me. A huge part of me wants to ask Abby where he is so I can punch the fucker in the face. But it's clear she doesn't need a hero. Abby knows how to take care of herself, but if I ever run into the asshole, I'll remind him if he ever talks to her like that again, he'll be eating my fist.

"You know that's not true, right?"

She slices the air with her hand. "Oh, I know. I mean, sure I'm curvy but I like my body. And damn, do I love food. Ben was having a bad moment, he didn't mean it. He certainly didn't think I'd ever leave. He's apologized hundreds of times since then. It was a weak move, and he knows it. Then my parents swooped in and helped me buy my house and furnish it. Stella and I ... we're really lucky."

I shift in my seat, feeling better that the loser apologized to her, and she has amazing parents. Still, I'll say my piece when I meet him. Because if I have my way, I'll be spending a lot more time with Abby and Stella.

Abby slices the air with her hand again. "Anyway, I don't want to talk about him anymore. I want to get lost in Rachel's paintings."

"That's what we're going to do, Stormy." I get out of the truck and make my way to the passenger side.

When I open it Abby says, "Speaking of food, after this are you up for something greasy? I'd kill for a burger, fries, and Diet Coke."

I reach behind her and grab her ass. Pressing our bodies together, I shield us from the frosty air. "Anything you want." I lean down, and plant a long, wet kiss on Abby's lips.

She moans, and playfully grabs my arm when I turn toward the door like she can't walk without my help. I wrap my arm around her shoulders, pull her into me, and kiss her forehead as we head inside.

"You really do know how to calm my stormy side, you know that?"

"Hearing you say that makes me really fucking happy, Abby."

The line at the entrance of the studio has disappeared, everyone scattered inside the large open building. When I open the door and place my hand on the small of Abby's back to guide her in, the scent of orange and clove in the air, she gasps and heads to the back wall. Her eyes are laser-focused on a painting. I follow her, my eyes floating over the crowd and paintings as I do. I've never seen a Rachel Turner painting in person, but when Abby told me she really wanted to go to the opening, I looked her up and damn, was I impressed. Rachel's abstract paintings are captivating online. But in person, the way the colors swirl into each other has a calming effect. I'm mesmerized, and can see why there was a line out the door when we got here.

Abby stops in front of a large painting, and I slide her long black coat from her shoulders, my eyes locked on the work of art. The white circle in the center of the piece is surrounded by bigger circles, the swirls going from ivory to light gray to dark gray. I want to reach out and touch it, the perfectly blended paint is textured like there was salt or sand added, and the birch frame sets it off perfectly.

"I love this," Abby says as she leans in closer to the painting, then pins me with her eyes. "It's like ... like a storm."

CHAPTER 12
Abby

Dylan wraps his hand around the back of my neck. "You took the words right out of my mouth, Stormy." My entire body relaxes under his touch, yet the tremble of desire ripples through me so strong I can't even fight it. Dylan makes me feel more like a woman than any man ever has.

His lips touch my ear and he whispers, "We still like that nickname, right?"

I try to say yes. Instead, I whimper.

"Should I assume that's a yes?" His fingers knead into the back of my neck, and I swear my body releases all the tension I've been carrying around since my divorce.

This night is so perfect, too perfect. I'm in Rachel Turner's studio surrounded by her amazing creativity. It smells like Christmas, and the simple trees wrapped with twinkle lights make me feel so happy and light that I could practically float away. The talk I had with Dylan on the way over felt like a cleanse. He really listened and as much as I love how he wants to help me fix things around my house, he doesn't try to fix me. I can be myself around him, and the feeling of comfort and arousal he gives me is a combination I've never known. I want to hang on to it, ball it up in my fists and hide it away somewhere safe and private so it never goes away.

I swallow and turn to face him. "That's a yes."

"Good," he says before dropping a kiss on the top of my head. "You keep looking around, and I'll be right back. I'm going to hang our coats up, use the bathroom then return to take this all in."

I rub the back of my neck, missing his touch as he walks away. Unable to drop the smile plastered on my face, I make my way around the studio. People are talking and laughing, glasses of wine and pink cocktails in their hands. The right side of the long marble bar displays a few charcuterie boards, one savory and one sweet. I make my way over and ask the bartender for a Diet Coke with light ice. Maybe I should splurge and get that painting. It's so stunning and would look fantastic over my fireplace. I've only allowed myself the basics since moving into my little house a year ago, seeing a piece like that every morning will be a great start to the day. And of course, it will remind me of this night.

I head to the center of the studio to look at it from afar, and my heart sinks when I see someone rush over to attach a "Sold" tag on the wall next to it. I strut across the room, trying not to slosh my soda, hoping that I'm seeing things.

I let out a sigh. My stormy painting has been sold only minutes after I decided I wanted it. I guess it's just as well. Even though tips are good during the holidays, I really shouldn't spend the money on it anyway. I haven't even started Christmas shopping for Stella yet.

When Dylan sidles up next to me, his face is flushed. "I got lost out there," he says, throwing a thumb over his shoulder. "You have to go through a maze to get to the bathroom."

"Good to know since I just sucked down this Diet Coke."

His dark eyes linger over my face. "What's wrong? You

look sad. Don't worry, after we leave, I'll get you a real soda. One that comes in a cup the size of a paper towel roll, not a sad, little Dixie cup."

"Oh, it's not the soda. Although, yes, please." I take Dylan's arm and turn his body toward the painting. "It sold. I was thinking about getting it."

He knits his eyebrows together, and his hand goes to the back of my neck again. "Well, let's keep looking. Maybe there's another you'd like?"

We stroll hand in hand through the studio twice. Every piece is absolutely beautiful, but nothing moves me like that first one. Now I'm determined to save some money and go to every one of Rachel's art openings to see if I can find another painting that makes me feel the same way. Yes, I loved that one, but nothing can ruin the magic that I feel tonight.

An hour later, my stomach rumbles so loud that I'm sure everyone can hear it over the hum of chatter and the Christmas jazz. Dylan says, "Okay, I'm starving. Are you ready to eat?"

"I am," I say, as Dylan grabs our coats from the coat rack next to the front door and drapes mine over my shoulders. When he opens the door, the crisp air takes my breath away. "Can we eat in your truck with the seat warmers on?"

"You read my mind," he laughs, pulling me next to him, doing everything he can to shield me from the cold.

After eating French fries and burgers in the truck as snowflakes fall and we talk about some of our favorite childhood memories, Dylan's face goes serious. When he traces his fingers down my neck, and asks what I'd like to do next, I say, "I think that's obvious, don't you? We should have sex. To see if we're compatible." My eyes fall to his crotch.

It's mostly a joke because based on the other night, we're

obviously compatible in that way. And seeing as I've had more fun tonight than any other date I've been on since my divorce, I'm so at ease that I can tell him anything.

But Dylan doesn't laugh. Fuck, he doesn't even smile. He just puts his truck in reverse, and his hand goes to the back of my neck again.

We make it through town in record time, and when he cuts the engine and lowers his hand to my upper thigh, he says, "You want to see if we're compatible?"

I uncross my legs, ready to take him now. The silence on the way home as he rubbed the back of my neck was all the foreplay I needed. There's nothing like a take-charge man who wants to show you how he can improve your life. And I'm ready for all the improvements Dylan has to offer. "I do." Part of me wonders if I should tell him that I'm kidding, that I already know we're a good match and if my inkling is right, the sex is going to be explosive.

But I like this game we're playing better. Much better.

His eyes are locked on his hand as it moves higher up my thigh, so close to my heat that I feel a gush between my legs. "I think you know we're fucking compatible and that I can treat you and handle you better than any man can. You like that I can calm that stormy side of you because I can take charge when you need me to. And right now, you want me to take charge of that beautiful pussy I ate the other night, don't you?"

I pull in a breath, speechless, and take Dylan's hand and put it between my legs. "I do," I say again, pressing my forehead to his.

"Then get that perfect ass inside. I'm going to show you, right under that Christmas tree I brought you, just how fucking compatible we are. In fact, I'm going to show you so good, you're never going to want another man to do a thing for you."

His fingers are barely touching me over the knit fabric of my dress. I'm aching, throbbing. One skin to skin touch and I'll unravel over his thick fingers.

Dylan is behind me as we fumble inside. He has one arm around my waist and slides his other hand into the V of my dress and finds my nipple. Sucking and kissing my neck, he presses his front to my back. I can barely think, barely see, as I get the key in the door and swing it open.

We somehow make it over the threshold without falling, a tangled mess as we rip and pull off each other's clothes. My purse and keys fall to the floor as Dylan helps me slip out of my dress. I peel off my boots and my entire body breaks out in goosebumps as he finishes taking off his jeans that I've undone. He slides off his underwear, and before I even look at what I know is a very fine cock, I reach for it.

When he straightens, his jaw clenches as his eyes travel over me. The Christmas tree illuminates the living room, and Dylan closes the gap between us and his fingers slip into my underwear. He covers his mouth with mine, and when he parts my folds, my fingers dig into the meat of his hard ass with my free hand.

Circling his finger over my wetness, he whispers, "You want me to calm this storm, don't you?"

I bite my bottom lip and nod. Our eyes lower together as we watch my hand glide over his thick cock, and his fingers circle over my swollen clit. My breath catches and I feel my orgasm building in my core.

Dylan groans. "Tell me what you want, Stormy. Do you want me to go faster?"

My entire body buckles under his touch, the waves of pleasure passing through me so fast all I can do is hold on to his hard cock for dear life. I contract and tremble under his hand as his fingers move over my sensitive bud at the perfect pace.

Dylan takes over for me, pulling on his cock with his free

hand as the last tremor runs through me. He's pleasuring me and pleasuring himself at the same time. If that's not a good man, then I don't know what is, although he's not going to do all the work. I want that amazing shaft inside me right this second.

We're slicked with sweat as I wrap my hand over his. Together, we stroke his dick. "We're so compatible. So fucking compatible," I say, my lips crash into his and he leads me to the Christmas tree.

When he pulls away to grab the blanket that's in a heap on my sofa, I slide off my underwear. "That's right, we fucking are," he says, grabbing my hand and leading me to the floor. "You get comfortable."

Our clothes are in a heap next to us and Dylan grabs his jeans and pulls out a condom, his leg and glute muscles pop as he makes his way back to me. Standing over me, a huge smile plastered on his chiseled face, he rolls the condom on. How is it that a twenty-seven-year-old can handle the whole protection thing flawlessly, and men in their forties show up without it, and complain about having to cover their dicks?

I'm on my back, propped up on my elbows as Dylan kneels between my legs, covered cock and all. "I'm ready," I purr.

"Are you sure?" he asks, scooting closer, his hard shaft in his hand.

I nod and tilt my hips up. Our eyes are locked when he slams into me, the fullness so intoxicating that I cry out. Dylan is on his knees, his fingers sink into my hips as he guides me in and out, my tits bounce in my pushup bra with each thrust.

"Fuck, you look so beautiful. Can you feel it? Can you feel how well we fit together?" Dylan asks, barely able to get the words out.

"Yes. My God, yes." The truth is, I do feel it. And it's not just his thick cock. It's how his eyes devour me. The way his hands hold on to my hips like he never wants to let me go. He's not just touching me in a physical way. I feel him in my heartbeat, deep in my bones, zinging through every nerve.

"Lie back," he whispers. I do as I'm told, my chest heaving. His command is so much hotter than suggesting we change positions.

Dylan lowers his upper body, throws my legs over his shoulders, then straightens to his knees again so my ass and hips are completely off the ground. His grip is tight on my hips and he pushes and pulls in and out of me under the Christmas tree I wouldn't have if it weren't for him, showing me just how capable he is of servicing me in every way.

Merry fucking Christmas to me.

CHAPTER 13
Abby

"Mom, you're seeing him again! You really like this guy." Stella sits on the edge of my bed, an oversized iced latte in her hand.

I pull down my tan cropped sweater, then turn to check out my butt in the mirror. "I do like him. Is this ... too much?"

Stella shakes her latte and shakes her head. "Nope, I love the brown leather leggings, Mom. You look great. And so ... happy since you've been hanging out with him."

"I am happy, honey." My skin tingles at the thought of Dylan. He'll be here in an hour, and I can't wait to go Christmas shopping with him. In the week that we've known each other, he's enhanced my life. Had I known he was out there, I wouldn't have wasted my time with any other men. The fact that Stella has already met him and is happy for me makes this so much easier. I've never introduced her to anyone I've dated, and it feels wonderful to have her approval. I couldn't imagine dating someone she didn't like, and although I'm pretty sure Ben isn't seeing anyone now, I know she's met a few of his past girlfriends. So far, she hasn't said much about anyone Ben has introduced to her to except saying they were "okay."

Stella sets her latte on her knee, her pajama pants and long blond ponytails reminding me of when she was younger. "I'm glad you're finally going Christmas shopping. I sent you my list again this morning. Did you get it?"

I laugh. "Yes, and I got it the first three times you texted it."

The knock at the door breaks her concentration, and she shoots up. "That's Dad! We're getting pizza then picking up Lauren." She runs out of my room and clomps down the stairs.

Ben is standing inside the front door when I make my way downstairs. Stella throws on her fleece and grabs her backpack that's at the bottom of the steps.

"Hello, Ben."

My ex-husband isn't shy about giving me a once over. "You look nice," he says, shoving his hands in his coat pockets.

"Yeah, she does! She has a date with Dylan!"

My heart skips a beat as Stella bends to get her backpack. I'm glad she's so comfortable sharing this information—it's certainly not a secret and I believe it's a sign of good co-parenting. The last thing Stella needs is to feel like she has to censor herself in front of her parents. But it's still a little strange to be discussing this with Ben.

His jaw clenches as Stella gives me a hug and kisses me on the cheek. "Bye Mom, have fun! I'll see you Sunday night!"

I squeeze my daughter and inhale her sweet coffee scent.

"Go ahead and wait in the car, honey," Ben says. I'll be out in a minute. "I left it running so you won't get cold." Stella whips her head, hitting me in the face with her hair as she does.

Ben's eyes haven't left me since I came downstairs, and

even though I was married to this man for seventeen years, I feel uneasy.

"I wanted to talk to you about that guy you're seeing." He widens his stance and crosses his arms. "Stella said he's like twenty-five or something?"

"He's twenty-seven. Yeah. And his name is Dylan." I'm immediately defensive, and I don't know why. I owe Ben nothing. He's dated a few women, even introduced them to Stella, and I never considered sticking my nose in his personal life or asking about their ages.

He scrubs his salt-and-pepper hair with his hands, and his pale face gets red and blotchy. "Have you thought about what's going to happen if this works out? He's closer to Stella's age than yours. I don't think I'm comfortable with that. When he's forty and you're almost sixty?" He smiles, but it doesn't reach his eyes. "You think he's going to want you then, Abby?"

My entire body tenses, and I tilt my chin up. "This isn't your concern, Ben. Go spend time with your daughter." I absolutely refuse to listen to him. He was wrong when he told me no one would want me, and he knows it. Even apologized for it. So why is he doing this? Why is he trying to tear me down in my own fucking house? It doesn't matter why, I won't allow it.

He holds his hands in the surrender position and takes a step backward. "Hey, I'm only concerned, trying to—"

I take a long stride to him. "I told you. Go spend time with your daughter." I blink twice, trying with all my strength to hold myself together.

The room spins as Ben's eyes travel over me once more before turning to leave.

I squeeze my eyes shut as he slams the door. My gut is heavy and I press my palm to the wall to keep my balance.

How can a few seconds with that man bring up so much

shit? Maybe I haven't thought this through? Maybe having him around Stella isn't the best idea. And I hate to admit that Ben is right about something: I am a lot older than Dylan. And he's so gorgeous, in great shape, and could have his pick of women. I'm only going to get older, and I'll never have a slender, toned body. Sure, he is interested in me now. But I didn't think that far into the future. Maybe I'm a challenge or he has childhood issues he is trying to work through via me. But I'll get saggy and probably curvier and while I can get away with it now, Dylan will still be smoking hot when he's forty and I'll be pushing sixty and fuck, I could save myself from future misery by not falling in love with him, breaking it off right now, and chalking this up to the holiday season that I had a fuckboy for a few weeks.

It certainly does make a great story. So maybe that's all this is and I need to accept it.

CHAPTER 14
Dylan

When I asked Abby if everything was okay after getting my text, she said it was, but something is off. I was supposed to pick her up to go Christmas shopping, but she insisted on coming to my place instead so we could talk.

In the few short relationships I've had, hearing "we need to talk " has never resulted in anything good, but I'm so excited to give Abby the painting I bought for her, I can't think about anything else. It's been hard to keep the secret, but instead of telling her, I want to see her face while she unwraps it. I thought I'd be able to bring it home with us on opening night, but the deal was that it had to stay in the studio until the end of the week.

I run around my house, giving all the rooms a once over. I like to keep things neat, and I'm rarely here, but I want to make sure it's in good shape since this is the first time Abby will see my place. I straighten the small pile of books on my coffee table then spread them out. On second thought, things can't be too perfect. I certainly don't want Abby to feel shitty because I can be a neat freak and her house is more ... lived in.

Matthew's truck pulls into my driveway, and I rush to the front door. "You're just in time, brother. My girl will be here soon, thanks for picking this up for me."

It's dark, but I see Matthew's smile under the light of the full moon. "Hey, no problem. I got there just before the studio closed. I'm guessing this gift is going to get you quite a bit of action?"

He slides the wrapped painting from the back of his van, and I shake my head. "It's not like that, man. This is a gift for a very special woman."

Matthew can be a hothead, but I've known him since high school with him and he's helped me out quite a bit. He doesn't like to be tied down to a woman or to a job, so he's the perfect person to call on when I need an extra set of hands or someone to run errands, He can be a prick though when it comes to women, so there's a huge disconnect between us.

Laughing, he heads toward me, and I grab one end of the painting. Absolutely nothing can happen to this. "Whatever you say, boss. Aren't you a little young to be so into one woman? Have you seen the talent out there? Especially this time of year you can really clean up. You should've seen—"

"Thanks, Matt," I interrupt. Usually I'd entertain him by listening to his stories. He's a self-proclaimed male whore and proud of it. But I don't have time for his shit today. I am thankful he helped me out though. There were a slew of calls earlier this week, and I can't leave my customers with broken stoves and refrigerators so close to Christmas. "I appreciate you doing this. When I saw your last appointment was a mile away, I hoped it wouldn't be a problem for you to pick it up."

"Happy to do it. Glad you called the other day, I needed the extra money for Christmas gifts."

"When are you going to come work for me full-time? Repairmen are hard to come by. There aren't many reliable guys out there who do what we do."

We carefully get the painting inside, and I lean it against the wall in the foyer. "Yeah, growing up poor and having to help my dad every time something broke has come in handy. But I told you, I'm not ready to commit to a job. Maybe in a few years?"

I stalk to my kitchen where my wallet sits on the countertop. "Well, by then I might find someone else." I take out the cash I got on the way home to pay him. "Although I know I said those exact words a few years ago when you denied me the first time."

Matthew reaches for the cash and stuffs it in his coat pocket. "That you did, Dylan. That you did." He turns and heads for the door. "I've got a date so I'll see you tomorrow?"

I'm relieved he's leaving so soon. Abby will be here in a few minutes and I can't decide if I should show her the painting as soon as she walks in or wait until after we talk. "Sounds good, I texted you the appointments, you get them?"

We step outside, the night air even colder than it was a few minutes ago. There's a car in the distance, and as it gets closer, I wonder what Abby wants to talk about. She said everything was okay, and things have been going so freaking amazing that I hope she's not having a change of heart over the age thing.

"I did, boss." Matthew slaps my arm. "Now I gotta get my pipes cleaned out if you know what I'm saying." We laugh and my eyes follow the headlights pulling into my driveway.

Abby parks right next to Matthew, and when he backs out of the driveway her head follows his van.

Taking quick steps to meet her at her car, I recognize the frazzled look on her face. It's the same one she had the night we met, the storm I was compelled to calm.

Her eyes lock with mine. Abby looks like she's been punched in the gut. *Shit, she really does need to talk.*

But when I reach for her car door handle she shakes her head and backs out of my driveway. It takes me a second to realize she's driving away. My arms pump, and the cold air stabs at my lungs as I run down the street calling her name.

After a few blocks, her taillights fade in the distance. I stop, rest my hands on my knees, and try to catch my breath. I need to come up with another plan, but my heart hurts knowing I'm never going to catch Abby if she doesn't want me to.

CHAPTER 15
Abby

My car accelerates as I head to my parents' house because, of course, I'm running to Mommy and Daddy, just like Rebecca says I always do. My hand goes to my chest, trying to soothe the pain that just ran through it.

I'm such an idiot to think that Dylan was different, that he was actually into me. I'm sure he and that asshat from the wedding got a good laugh at how he banged me under the Christmas tree that he bought. I can picture Neck Tattoo congratulating him on such an epic move.

I swerve to the side of the road and park as sobs force their way out before tears form. Dialing Lila's number, I paw around in my car for a tissue. I find one in the center console, and as soon as she picks up, I blow my nose.

"Um, hello? Abby?" Lila is breathless again because, of course, she is. Her relationship is new, so it's a bone fest all the freaking time. God, I love that stage.

I squeeze my eyes shut and grip my steering wheel. "I'm sorry, Lila. Are you riding Holt again?"

"Ha, no. I'm carrying Christmas gifts up the stairs to hide

in my closet, but that's next on the list so make it snappy," she says under a giggle.

Getting to the point is my superpower. Lila knows this about me, so what I'm about to tell her won't surprise her. No sense in holding back. After all, she needs to go have sex with her amazing man. I hate my life.

"I just left Dylan's house. He was standing in front of his house giving a high five to that shitbag of a man who got my number at Ivory's wedding."

"Hold up. The waiter? The one who had a bet with his friend?"

"Yes!" I cry, unable to control myself. The tears are flowing now and I feel like the biggest nimrod. I want to go home, crawl under my covers, and tune tonight out. I hate that Ben was right. I hate that I was so naïve. And I hate that I believe there could ever be anything between me and Dylan. Dylan with the fabulous dick. Dylan with the dark eyes. Dylan with the—

"Well, why was he there? What did he say when you asked him?"

I cover my eyes with my hand and shake my head as if that will erase what I just witnessed. "I didn't ask him! He was there congratulating Dylan on the fact that he won first prize in the Secret Cougar Banging Club!"

There's rustling in the background. "Okay, Abby. Calm down, your voice is very high right now. You aren't driving, are you?"

"No! I'm not a total idiot."

"Of course you aren't. But what are you talking about? A secret club?"

"The secret club of which twenty-something can get into an old lady's pussy first!" I yell. "Apparently, Dylan takes things to the extreme. Really knows how to fool a single mother like me who's so desperate for love and affection, she falls for all of his tricks."

"Abby, I don't think you are being ... rational right now—"

"Rational? You want me to be rational? I've been played by two men weeks before Christmas, I haven't even started my shopping yet, and all my fucking pants are too tight! Being rational isn't in the cards for me this season. Fuck!"

"If you didn't talk to Dylan, how do you know that they are doing the secret club thing? Maybe he knows him through work or something. Leeds Falls is a small town, Abby. Don't jump to conclusions. Does he know you saw them together? Not to mention just the idea of a club is, well, too stupid to be believable."

I blow my nose again. "Oh, he knows! Mother fucker tried chasing me down the street. Probably already had some stupid-ass story to cover up his antics. Men like that, Lila, they aren't used to getting caught. Or being outsmarted."

"He chased you down the street? In your moving car? It's like ten below zero out there."

I've calmed down enough to pull back onto the road. "Oh, stop being on his side, Lila."

"I'm on your side. Which is why I'm going to tell you to listen to what he has to say. I guarantee he's already called you a few times since you sped away. And from what you've told me, Dylan is a confident man who knows what he wants. His business has a great reputation. Ask yourself if he's really capable of doing what you're accusing him of."

Dylan has tried to call and has sent several messages since I raced out of there on two wheels. I guess chasing after me accounts for something. I pull in a long breath. "Ben came over to get Stella, and ... he said a few things that got to me."

"Like?"

"Oh, you know, that I'm an old hag and I need to think

about having this young guy around Stella, and that I'll be practically sixty when Dylan is forty."

"That prick! He's just mad because he lost you. His balls are starting to look like two rocks in the toe of a pair of pantyhose. He's projecting his fear of aging on you. Why are you listening to him? He hasn't been able to handle the fact that you left him, and he's trying to bring you down. You know he's a toxic narcissist. Don't you see, Abby? You're in your head. Stop telling yourself this story. In fact, stop making any kind of assumptions until you talk to Dylan."

Leave it to Lila to say something hysterically funny nestled in the middle of her bits of wisdom. "I'll try," I say, pulling into my parents' driveway. A flicker of nostalgia pools in my belly when I see their Christmas tree through the window. My dad always insisted on big, honking colorful lights and even though he and Mom would argue about it every year, Mom would let him have his way.

"Don't try. Do it. Talk to him, then call me back."

"Maybe you're right," I say under a sigh as I get out of my car.

"You know I'm right, Abby. I want a full report."

I head toward the front porch, and the frosty air stings my flushed cheeks. "You go have a humping sesh. I'm going to gather myself, then I'll call Dylan back. Love you."

I slide my phone into my purse just as my parents open their front door. They are wearing matching T-shirts that say "This is my Christmas movie watching T-shirt." Definitely Mom's idea.

Dad takes one look at my face and rushes me. "Abigail, what is it?" Folding me in his arms, he walks me through the door and my tears start flowing again.

"Gracious, dear, what is it?" Mom asks, taking my hand.

Snot slides out of my left nostril, and I gasp for air. "Man problems. Why is this so hard?"

Even though I know Lila is right, and I need to at least hear Dylan out before I jump to conclusions, I'm tired, spent. I'm having one of those moments when being a single mom, and doing life alone is stripping me of everything.

Mom and Dad are my soft place to land. And being here means I can let loose and be dramatic. I need to at least get the rest of this emotional buildup out of my system, then I'll get their opinion on this whole debacle before I call Dylan.

CHAPTER 16
Dylan

Abby's house is dark, and her car isn't in her driveway like I'd hoped. I'll fucking wait all night if I have to. I don't know why Abby sped away like she did. I think she was only in my driveway for a total of twenty seconds. There's no way she mistook Matthew for another woman, the guy looks like he walked out of an issue of *GQ*.

My truck engine roars to life and I blast the heat. I might be here for a while, and it's getting cold fast. It's obvious we aren't going to get any Christmas shopping done, but now that I have the painting that Abby fell in love with on our first date, nothing will stop me from giving it to her.

Scrubbing my face with my hands, I search for some clue I may have missed. I sent Abby a text first thing this morning, and we chatted throughout the day. She was her usual flirty self and was excited about tonight. She messaged me before she left for work, and then I didn't hear from her until I got her text telling me that we needed to talk and she'd be coming to my place instead.

I grab my phone to read our text thread. Maybe I missed something? My thumb slides over my screen and I smile at the selfie she sent me this morning. I love her energy and honestly, I've been thinking about walking through the mall, hand in hand, then taking her home and fucking her under her tree again.

Shaking my head, I see I really haven't missed anything. I sent her my address, asked her if everything was okay, and tried to call several times, but she wouldn't pick up.

I may not know what's going on in her head, but if she thinks I'm just going to walk away because she's had a stressful day, she's wrong. I've apparently done something to upset her so we're going to talk about it like adults and come to an understanding. If Abby doesn't want to see me anymore, she's going to have to be very clear about that. I'll respect her wishes, of course, but I really don't think that's the issue here. I'm just a man who has no idea what she's actually thinking about or going through.

I hear a car approaching and headlights cast a glow inside my truck. I blow out a breath when Abby pulls in the driveway. I'm a patient man, but these last few hours of not knowing what the fuck is going on wasn't comfortable, and I'm anxious to resolve it.

I haven't been with a lot of women, but one thing Mom taught me was that it's best, in all your relationships, to confront things so you can move past them. She reminded me often that people usually regret the things they don't do, not the things they do. Sure, I could ignore Abby's behavior and wait for her to come to me. But that's not going to happen. That woman is in her masculine energy enough as a single mom.

When she opens her car door, I grab the top of it and open it the rest of the way. "Abby, what's going on?"

Dried tears streak her cheeks, and there are black smudges under her eyes. She steps out of her car, her hooded eyes lower. "Dylan, I'm so sorry. I had ... I was having a moment. Ben came over and said some things, then I saw you with that ... guy."

Abby's teeth chatter, and she crosses her arms over her chest. I reach out and grab her furry coat sleeve and lead her inside. "Okay, take a breath. Let's go inside and talk."

What did her ex-husband say to make her run from me? If he made her cry, I'll fucking punch his lights out. And Matthew? What's the connection there? My mind is racing with questions, but my first order of business is to get Abby inside where it's warm so we can sit down and figure this out.

Abby plops down on her sofa and wraps her long coat around herself. A faint smile crosses her lips but her eyes are sad. I sit down next to her and place a hand on her knee.

She shakes her head. "I ... I'm sorry. I should have asked you this earlier instead of leaving your house. But, how do you know that guy?" She winces, like she's watching a disturbing scene in a movie.

"Matthew?" It's odd to me that she's so curious about him, and that he obviously has a negative effect on her. I want to know what happened, but it's more important to just answer her question instead of making her even more anxious than she already is.

"I went to high school with him. We've never hung out or anything, we ran in different circles, but he helps me out here and there. I've been trying to get him to work for me, but he's a free spirit. Doesn't like to be tied down."

Abby chews on her bottom lip, and her eyes fall to my hand that's caressing her knee. "So, you two aren't ... playing games with me?"

My hand stops. "Huh?" This evening is getting stranger by the second, but when Abby's big blue eyes crinkle at the edge and a laugh bubbles out of her, all I can think about is how vulnerable and sexy she is.

"He asked me out a few weeks ago at a wedding."

"Oh," I say, feeling my pulse quicken. I don't like the sound of this at all. Matthew is a hard worker, but when it comes to women, he's a complete asshole. "And?"

Abby leans back into the sofa cushions and wrings her hands together. "Well, he asked me out, but it was a joke, a bet with one of his friends to get my number because I'm a lot older. And ... voluptuous. I heard him talking about me right after I took his phone and put in my number. I was the fifty-dollar prize for the evening."

My jaw clenches and I shoot up from the sofa. "What? I knew he was a dick, but I didn't know he pulled shit like that. I'll fucking set him straight, Abby. And you know that says nothing about you. You are—"

She yanks my hand and pulls me back down. "It's fine, Dylan. I mean, it's not *fine*. It was incredibly cruel, and I threw a delicious piece of chocolate cake in the trash for him which was a huge waste."

My fists clench. "It's not fine, Abby. I will never associate with him again. I want nothing to do with him. He hurt your feelings, I can find someone else to help me out. And I can't have someone working for me who acts like such a pig. Who knows if he's been inappropriate with some of my customers."

"Oh, like taking my hand and leading it into the hole of my rubber ring wasn't appropriate?" Abby throws her head back in a laugh. "I appreciate you getting all worked up though. It's hot."

I grab her in a hug. "So, is that what happened? You thought we were in a secret club to get in your pants?"

Her arms wrap around me, and she nuzzles into my neck. "For a minute, I did, Yes. It seems so stupid now. And pretty fucking arrogant."

I cradle the back of her head. "But that's not the whole story, Abby. Something else happened because you canceled our plans for tonight. You said we needed to talk." I'm relieved she's feeling better, but I don't want to ignore what made her change her mind. Besides, isn't ignoring a woman's request that she wants to talk about something a death wish?

"Ben came over. He got to me about our age difference. He said when you were forty and I was almost sixty you wouldn't want me. Then I realized we've only started dating and there's no need to overthink this. Who knows what will happen."

Now there's two men I need to punch in the nose. I squeeze her tighter. Abby is a gift and her ex-husband knows it. Otherwise, he wouldn't be trying to get in her head, trying to knock her down. "Well, we don't know what's going to happen. Losing my mom taught me that. But Abby, I do want to explore this with you. I think you are amazing and exciting. You certainly keep me on my toes and you are the sexiest woman I've ever met. And if I'd be so lucky to be with a woman like you until I'm forty, the age gap would be insignificant. Just like Matthew and Ben's opinions. Do you hear me?"

Abby pulls away and her eyes hold mine before she drops her gaze. Nodding she says, "I hear you. I do. I had a ... revelation tonight." Her voice is soft, almost a whisper. "After I left your house, I went to see my parents. To, you know, feel sorry for myself and be dramatic. It's what I've done my entire life, but especially since my divorce, I've leaned on my parents too much."

I tuck a strand of blond hair behind her ear. "It's good to have people to count on. And you're lucky to have them."

Abby shakes her head. "No, it's ... it's more than that. Yes, my divorce was hard, but I've played the victim. Complained about how hard life is and used it as an excuse to run late all the time, and ask my parents for more help than I actually needed. My sister has called me out on it a few times, and she's right."

Tears wet her eyes, and I want so much to tell her to stop

being so hard on herself, that she's not doing anything wrong by leaning on her parents. But I don't because Abby isn't asking me for advice. She doesn't need me to fix her. She needs me to keep my mouth shut so she can finish her thoughts.

"I don't want to be that ... pathetic person anymore. I shouldn't have run away from you tonight, and I shouldn't have let Ben get to me. I'm sorry. You must think I'm crazy."

Okay, now I'm going to open my mouth. "Abby, I don't think you're crazy. I think you have a lot on your plate and you worry. I think you love Stella with everything you have, but it's hard when she's here because it's all on you, and it's hard when she leaves because you miss her so damn much. And I think you worry. A lot. You don't get a break from worrying when she's gone, either. Your ex-husband didn't deserve you, and you have to keep that relationship healthy for Stella's sake no matter what that prick says and that's incredibly difficult. And I can't imagine what that does to a person."

Abby's lips part, and a sound escapes her throat. Her watery eyes travel over my face. "Dylan, I ... no one has ever ... where the fuck did you come from?"

CHAPTER 17
Abby

"Abby, I don't think you are crazy. I think you have a lot on your plate and you worry. I think you love Stella with everything you have, but it's hard when she's here because it's all on you, and it's hard when she leaves because you miss her so damn much. And I think you worry. A lot. You don't get a break from worrying when she's gone, either. Your ex-husband didn't deserve you, and you have to keep that relationship healthy for Stella's sake no matter what that prick says and that's incredibly difficult. And I can't imagine what that does to a person."

That. That right there is the moment I fall in love with Dylan. I'm trying to soak this moment in, let his words sink into the deep parts of me that believe I don't deserve a man who thinks this way and says these things.

"Dylan, I ... no one has ever ... where the fuck did you come from?"

He cradles my face in his hands, his dark eyes lock with mine. "I hope you know how much I mean that. And how pitiful I think it is that other men set the standard so low that me seeing you, really seeing you, is so rare. It should be the standard. And I guess men like Matthew give us a bad name, but it's never an excuse. I'll never give you excuses, Abby. I can promise you that."

There are so many words and emotions trying to force their way out of me, I can't get behind any of them. I want to say so much, but I don't know where to begin. My mouth crashes into Dylan's, an impulse I can't control. Our tongues meet, his hands still holding my face, and I'm filled with a thirst only Dylan can quench.

I pull at the neck of his sweater and he reaches and lifts it over his head. Grabbing the hem of my sweater, I do the same until Dylan takes over. Getting out of these brown leather leggings isn't going to be graceful, but no amount of Spandex can keep me from this man. And I love how I'm not worried about how my thighs will jiggle when they spring free from the fabric, or if my belly rolls show when I bend over to free these pants from my ankles. Dylan is here for it all, devouring me with hungry eyes as he studies every inch of me and licks his lips.

I'm standing over him as he sits on the sofa, shirtless, his rugged hands tracing my curves like I'm a glass vase. "Take off your jeans," I say just as his fingers trickle down my heat, causing so much blood to flow there that I feel a gush of moist warmth.

He smiles and lies back on my sofa, his hooded eyes traveling up and down my body as he undoes his jeans and slides them down with his boxer briefs. His face is illuminated by my Christmas tree, his devilish smile growing wider as he pulls on his thick shaft. "This isn't just from you standing in front of me naked, looking like a goddess sent down from above especially for me. Stormy, it's from kissing you, from our intimate conversation, the feeling you give me every fucking time I see you."

Planting my legs on either side of Dylan, I straddle him.

He pulls in a breath when he feels my wetness on his cock, which I love. I want him to know what he does to me. Taking control is ingrained in this man's soul. It's not something he does to show off, or get something in return. This is just the way Dylan is. His maturity and self-assurance is so sexy, and is by far greater than any man I've ever been with.

I flip my hair over my shoulder as Dylan reaches behind me and undoes my bra. When the straps slide down my shoulders, he sits up and cups my tits in his hands. "Baby, you're so fucking beautiful."

Watching as he takes a nipple in his mouth, and rolls the other between his thumb and forefinger, I squirm on his hard dick. I grab the top of his head, my hips moving faster as he nibbles and sucks on me. "Fuck, Stormy, I'm gonna come before I'm even in you. Let me get a condom."

I grind harder, the sensation on my wet, swollen click takes over my body. "I don't want to stop, you feel so good. And I'm on birth control." I barely get out the words, but when I do, his fingers dig into my full ass and he guides his perfect cock inside me.

Burying his face into my neck as I lift myself up, then slide back down, he whispers, "You feel so fucking good."

The low rumble of his voice, and his cock filling me makes me feral. I place my palms on his chest and push him down on the sofa. Dylan has a sexy smirk as he watches me bounce up and down, telling me how much he loves this side of me. I love it, too. The old Abby, the one who leaned on her parents too much, didn't take control of her life, and settled for less, is gone.

I can't take my eyes off of Dylan as I ride him. I'm taking control, shedding old parts of myself as he stiffens underneath me. My entire body is tingling when Dylan parts me with two fingers, then rubs me with my own wetness until I come undone.

My body is so ready for release that my legs go numb when the first surge of rapture takes over my body. Dylan and I move together, our orgasms exploding inside me, and my face heats.

When he pulls me down on top of him and wraps his hefty arms around me, I fight the urge to tell him then and there that I could really fall in love with him. I know that I'm not just wrapped up in the lusty sex either. My heart feels different, I feel different.

Dylan's fingers trace my spine, and I release all my weight onto him. Our sweaty bodies are pressed together and we're still joined when he says. "I have something for you. Something I think you're going to like."

"Mm, I think you just gave me something I really like. I don't need anything else." I close my eyes, never wanting to leave his broad chest, never wanting his hands to stop touching me.

After a half hour, I finally pull myself off of Dylan. He can't stop talking about this thing he wants to give me, and it wouldn't be a bad idea to get something to eat since it's going on nine o'clock and we're both starving.

I lie on the sofa completely naked as Dylan pulls on his jeans. I whimper and grab his crotch when he zips them up. "Oh, we'll have round two after I make you something to eat. You said you had eggs and bacon, right? We can do breakfast for dinner."

"That sounds amazing. And tomorrow, we'll get up first thing and get all our shopping done?"

Dylan leans over and plants a long, soft kiss on my forehead. "You got it. Maybe you can help me pick out a gift for Stella? I'd like to get her a little something."

"Okay, that's so sweet of you."

Dylan pulls on his sweater, then reaches for the throw blanket that landed on the floor during our epic session, shakes it out, then covers me up before heading out of the room.

I stare at the ceiling, feeling like I'm floating. Dylan is the man for me. My washing machine broke at the perfect time, because if it had been anyone else but Marge sitting in my chair that evening, or if it had happened when I was home, I never would've met him.

Just when I don't think this evening could get any better, Dylan comes back inside, a smile across his face like I've never seen before, and presents me with a huge gift wrapped in white paper and tied with a white silk ribbon.

Lifting myself from the warm sofa, I wrap the blanket over my shoulders. "What is it?" I have no idea what it could be, but Dylan is so excited. Maybe it's some fancy piece for an appliance? A mirror? Oh, I bet it's some cheesy Christmas decoration for the outside because I didn't do a thing to decorate my yard for the holidays.

"Open it!" He holds it in front of me, and I laugh at how carefully he's handling it because it's the opposite of how he just handled me.

I purse my lips, and my toes curl. Pulling one end of the ribbon, I watch it fall to the ground.

"Okay, a little faster, please." He tosses his head back in a laugh.

All I can see is Dylan's face popping over the gift as he holds it in front of him. He looks like a kid who's entered a candy store for the first time, "Okay, I don't know where to rip into it though. It's wrapped so tightly and it's ... so big."

He gently sets it down on the floor, leaning it against his body as he feels around for the edge of the paper. "Oh here, I'll get it started." His thumb makes a tiny rip in the side and I take hold of the paper and pull, revealing a sliver of my gift.

I don't know how I didn't figure it out as soon as he brought it in, but when I see a glimpse of the painting I fell in love with the other night, my breath catches and every ounce of caution leaves my body. I tilt my chin up to find Dylan's teary eyes waiting for me to say something. "The storm! I love it so much, Dylan, I ... I love you."

"Abby, I love you." His eyes glisten. I haven't even seen the entire painting, but I don't need to. All I can see is Dylan, all I can feel is the love between us. And loving him has been the easiest decision I've made in a really long time.

Abby

EPILOGUE

One Year Later

The scent of baked ham fills the house as I step into my white leather dress. A short, strapless number isn't exactly traditional, especially on Christmas Eve in Maine, but I've never been traditional. After all, I'm in love with a man who's almost twenty years younger than me, and I like the fact that we turn heads in public.

I even had a client ask me what my son did for a living after she saw us together at Noah's Hardware. I took a little too much pleasure in whispering that he wasn't my son, that I was just having sex with him. It wasn't true, of course, Dylan and I share so much more than sex. He's my teammate, a true partner, and I don't doubt for a second that he'd do anything for me. Not that I need him to, because this past year I've realized exactly how much I can do for myself. And damn, I love this new version of me. Plus, having a smoking hot man by my side who's gentle with my heart and can toss me around in bed is the best bonus a woman could ask for.

I run my palms down the cool fabric and step into my gold stilettos. I love the way leather hugs my curves and my boobs look great in this dress if I do say so myself. In fact, the way the top of this dress accentuates my breasts is the reason I splurged on this the day after Dylan and I decided to plan this Christmas Eve party and invite everyone we know.

Stella and Dylan will be back soon with dozens of buttermilk biscuits that we ordered from Patty's Place, and everyone else will be here soon after that. Dylan has everything planned: he got up early to put in the ham, told everyone if they were even a second late to not even bother coming inside, and he insisted on Patty's homemade biscuits and peach preserves.

Lila and I transformed the living room into a snow globe last night, and my mom and dad dropped off an assortment of Christmas cookies which I arranged on white platters this morning while listening to Christmas jazz, thinking about how truly lucky I am to be surrounded with such love and generosity.

Dylan has been a bundle of nerves these past few days, but I know it's only because he wants everything to be perfect for me. I keep telling him it already is, and whatever happens today will be just right. Unless I fall down the stairs. Or someone chokes on a piece of ham. Or one of my parents has a heart attack and falls to their knees in front of the fireplace as we exchange our vows.

I close my eyes, shutting off the part of my brain that always thinks the worst. I've gotten so much better at this, but fuck it's a hard habit to breakeven on the day I'm getting married to the man of my dreams, surrounded by everyone I love most in the world.

I sit on the edge of my bed and look out the window. Frosty pine trees blur in my vision as I go over what I'm going to say to Dylan as we stand in front of the fireplace and exchange our vows. We thought about writing them down, but for some reason, I thought it would be more fun to be spontaneous and say whatever is on our minds at the moment since the rest of this day is going to be such a surprise for everyone else. Except Stella, of course. We had to tell my daughter we were going to have a surprise wedding on Christmas Eve as soon as Dylan presented me with the idea a few weeks ago.

It's been hard to keep the secret, especially from my parents, Lila, and Ivory. But everyone still seems to think they are just coming over for a regular ol' Christmas party.

Laughing, my belly flutters because I can't wait to see everyone's faces when I waltz down my stairs in this dress carrying a little bouquet of winter berries wrapped in white velvet ribbon. Will they know then what's going to happen?

When I hear Dylan's truck pull in the driveway, I stand, then plop back down. My mouth goes dry and I try to regulate my breathing. Up until this point, I was as calm as can be, but my pounding heart seems to be making up for lost time.

"We're home, Mom!" Stella's voice is followed by loud clomps and I can picture her and Dylan racing up the stairs. "How does the dress look?" she asks, breathless.

"It looks good, do you want to see?" I stand back up and wring my hands together.

"I need to get ready first! Then yes, I want to see! Are you wearing the heels?"

I take a few steps toward the door. "I am, yes. Are they ... too much?"

Dylan bursts into the bedroom, and I put my hands on my hips. "Dylan, you aren't supposed to see me. Your suit is in the downstairs bathroom! You need to get ready!"

His eyes fall to half-moons. "I know." Gently shutting the door behind him, he comes toward me. "I couldn't wait to see my bride. My soon-to-be wife. My Stormy." He pulls me to him and presses his mouth to mine. His kiss is hard, possessive, claiming me one last time before he turns to gentle Dylan in front of our guests. Pressing his forehead to mine, he says. "This dress. My fucking God, Stormy."

He slips a finger between my breasts and I close my eyes. It's a tight squeeze, but he grazes a finger across one of my pebbled peaks and I moan. "Dylan, everyone will be here soon." I playfully try to pull away even though I want nothing more than to feel his hands all over me. "It was a lot of work getting into this dress."

He retrieves his hand and groans. "You're right, my love. I'll behave. For now. But later, and I don't care how much work it is, this amazing dress is going to get lifted and you're going to bend over for me in front of that mirror"—he points to the full-length mirror leaning on the back wall—"so I can watch myself make love to my wife."

The sound of him calling me his wife makes my stomach somersault, and my eyes fill with tears as I wrap my arms around his neck. "Dylan, you have no idea how excited I am to be your wife. And I can't wait for you to be my husband. This last year ... you've made everything feel so right ... so easy." I blink back tears, not wanting to ruin my makeup.

But when Dylan says, "That's all on you, Stormy. Loving you has felt like the most natural thing I've ever done in my life," the tears flow. Being in the moment with a man who loves me unconditionally is much more important than perfect makeup.

"I can't wait to love you for the rest of my life," I say, knowing that's exactly how I'm going to spend today, and every day from now on.

∼

Want more? You're in luck!
Visit http://katiebinghamsmith.com for information on all of her novels. While you're there, join Katie's newsletter and get sexy bonuses not available anywhere else.

∼

Sometimes the one that got away is the only one worth fighting for. First loves find new flames in this small town second-chance romance. **Read on for a sneak peek of *Before She Knew*, the first novel in the Falling Leaves series!**

Before She Knew
FALLING LEAVES, BOOK 1

Sometimes the one that got away is the only one worth fighting for. First loves find new flames in this small town second-chance romance. For fans of Lucy Score.

∽

CHAPTER 1
Rachel

"Honey, take these things out of your ears and focus." Rachel reached across the kitchen island and tugged the earbuds out of her son's ears. "Listening to music will not help you get your math done any faster."

"Mom! Be careful with those! Aunt Emily just gave them to me. Besides, I work better when I listen to music." Benjamin raked his hands through his blond hair that stood up on the top of his head. The sides were shaved into a fade, and he preferred the top to be a spiky mess. His freckles were dwindling, along with the bit of padding he had left in his cheeks.

"Not according to your grades, Benny. Come on. I know you can do this." Rachel rested her elbows on the pile of towels she'd thrown on the island to fold, studying her son. Now that he was thirteen, it seemed like everything was too much work for him.

Trying to get him to do homework was becoming a daily chore, and Rachel wanted to lie in the warm pile of towels and say, "Okay, fine. Don't do it. I give up." Her throat was scratchy, and her shoulders ached. Was she coming down with something? She put the back of her hand against her forehead to see if she had a fever.

Elsa walked into the kitchen, opened the fridge, and filled her arms with a package of sliced turkey, mustard, and a bottle of water as their Golden Retriever, Cora, panted at her feet, hoping a scrap would fall. "I can help you, Ben." She turned and nudged the fridge door shut with her heel. "I had Mr. Chase in 8th grade for math too."

"Cool," Benjamin said, reaching for his earbuds, which were sitting next to the pile of laundry.

"Not with these, Mister!" Rachel said, grabbing them from his hands. She took a step over to her daughter and hugged her from behind.

Elsa was taller than Rachel and built exactly like her father; long and lean. "Thank you, Sweetie. I appreciate you helping your brother with math. You have a lot of patience." She smoothed the back of her daughter's long brown hair. "Lord knows I have little of it."

Elsa may have gotten Adam's long and lean body type, but she'd gotten Rachel's brown hair, olive skin, and brown eyes. It was a total mystery where she got her patience from.

"Mom, stop," Elsa said, half laughing as she shimmied from Rachel's embrace.

Elsa sat next to Benjamin, scooting her brown leather barstool closer to him before she plopped down her water and snack. Benny shoved his paper toward her, and Elsa studied the sheet.

Rachel felt a wash of relief as she grabbed a towel and folded it. Elsa was mostly out of her moody teen years and didn't hide in her room as much. Now it was Benjamin's turn. Lately, Elsa had been an enormous help with him, and Rachel was so happy the two weren't going through that difficult stage at the same time.

Elsa took the pencil from her brother's hand. "You're on the right track—you just keep forgetting to simplify the result to get the variable value. Then you can check your answer by plugging it back in to see if it works." She slid the paper back to her brother and picked up her phone.

Rachel didn't understand a word her daughter had just said. "You two sure didn't get your math skills from me," Rachel said, mating a pair of socks and rolling them into a ball. "Thank your father for that one."

"What are you talking about, Mom? I suck at math," Benjamin said, grabbing a piece of turkey and dangling it over his mouth before dropping it on his tongue. He grabbed the mustard from his sister's hand and squirted it into his mouth.

"Hey! Easy on the mustard." Rachel threw the ball of socks on the island. "And don't do that. Get some bread and make a sandwich."

"Too much work," Benjamin said, his mouth full of turkey. "I didn't touch it with my mouth."

Rachel opened her mouth to protest, but stopped herself when Benjamin picked up his pencil and got to work. Elsa smiled beside him as she tapped away on her phone.

They're fine. He's getting his work done without a meltdown. Leave it alone.

Rachel crossed "deep clean kitchen" off her to-do list. Yesterday, she'd scrubbed the subway tile backsplash that reached the ceiling. Then, she'd taken all the dishes off the open shelving and wiped the shelves down with her homemade potion of water, organic dish soap, and a few drops of lavender oil before mopping the floors. A clean kitchen made her ridiculously happy, and there was no way she had the energy to tackle it today.

She stared at the rest of the list, hoping another Diet Coke would get her through the rest of the evening. There was a painting to finish, dinner to make, and one more load of laundry to catch up on. She grabbed a can from the fridge and popped it open, feeling the fizz tickle her fingers. The carbonation felt wonderful on her raw throat.

"*Moommm*, easy on the Diet Cokes," Benjamin said in his best Mom voice without looking up from his work.

Rachel bent over to pick up the laundry basket, then got tunnel vision when she stood up too fast. Her clogged ears thumped behind her eyes, and she leaned against the island until everything came into focus. She took another swig of soda before heading to the laundry room to throw in one last load.

Get through tonight and go to bed early. As she shoved the whites into the dryer, she felt the dreaded nasal drip creeping down the back of her throat. Elsa used to call it "hot slime" when she was little and was coming down with a cold.

Rachel headed upstairs to get the Neti pot from the hall closet and as she opened it, the once neatly folded towels spilled out. She caught them just in time and shoved them back in place, then sorted through the bottles of medicine and extra shampoo and conditioner.

"Kids, do you know where my Neti pot is?" Yelling burned her throat, and she clutched her neck and leaned against the shelves.

All she got in response was laughter. "Hello?!"

"Benny and Hank used it to do the Diet Coke and Mentos explosion!" Elsa yelled. "Diet Coke and Mentos explosion" was muffled, and Rachel knew Benjamin was trying to cover her mouth with his hand.

"Stop, you idiot." A slapping sound made Rachel shake her head.

"I told you to put it back when you were done," Elsa said.

Rachel shook her head and popped a few Advil before walking back downstairs.

"Sorry, I don't remember where we put it." Benjamin smiled widely, keeping his teeth together. "Maybe in my room?"

"Well, I'm not going in there to look for *anything*." Rachel sighed and put her hands on her hips. "Okay, are you good here? I'm going to finish that painting for Joanna's mom." She took Benjamin's earbuds and tucked them into her pocket, and grabbed her can of soda. "You can have these back when you're done. And feed Cora please." She tousled his hair as she passed him, and he ducked away from her touch.

Rachel's "studio" was a corner in their finished walkout basement, where the kids always headed as soon as they had a friend over. The white leather sleeper-sofa they'd gotten from Ikea was perfect for when they had sleepovers, and Rachel always smiled when she saw the tiny bite marks Cora had taken out of a brown and ivory cowhide rug she'd tucked under the sofa.

She'd never put curtains or shades on the two small windows and glass door that led outside. She wanted as much light down there as possible. Something about dark rooms made her toes curl.

Each time Rachel went down there, she'd retrieve her painting supplies from the closet, set everything up, then put it all away when she was done. She dreamed of having a real painting studio with large windows, easels set up everywhere, and shelves that held every color of paint. In rainbow order, of course.

Her new neighbor, Joanna, had gone crazy over the navy blue and orange abstract painting Rachel had done for Benjamin's room. Rachel had given her a tour of their home after she'd come over to meet the family, and Joanna had stopped in her tracks as soon as she saw it. "Oh, can I commission you to make one just like that for me? I *have* to have it." Now Joanna's mother wanted a painting the same size, but requested neutrals—Rachel's favorite color palette—and "some kind of nature scene."

Before starting, Rachel sat down with the half-finished canvas in front of her and closed her eyes. *You should be in bed, but you promised you'd do this.* Joanna had reminded her this morning that her mother was hoping to have the painting done for her annual fall harvest party, which was this weekend.

Yesterday, she'd swirled browns and tans together across the entire canvas to create a moody sunset, and let it dry overnight.

It needs trees. She squirted tiny dots of black paint along the bottom of the canvas, then took a ruler to spread the paint about three quarters of the way to the top.

After taking a few steps back, she smiled—the black lines resembled tree shadows stretching up to the sky.

The hum of Benjamin and Elsa talking made its way downstairs. She stopped painting and tried to listen in. They could be a handful, but mostly, her kids were great friends. There was nothing that made her feel more at peace than witnessing their friendship.

As Rachel continued painting, the Advil kicked in and

took the edge off her cold. She made the trees a bit taller and painted in some clouds by adding a few white paint blobs to the sky, then blotted them with a sponge.

Joanna had said her mom loved fireflies, which inspired Rachel to take a small brush, dip it in gold paint, and flick it gently over the entire canvas.

She nodded her head after a few shakes of her brush, then reached for her Diet Coke. It was warm and had lost its fizz. A few hours to herself where she could get lost in her creativity always gave her new life.

Slowly standing up to admire her work, she let out a sigh and gathered her paints. She put them back in the closet, in rainbow order, and brought her brushes, sponges, and ruler up to be washed.

Until your next session.

Adam was standing at the kitchen island when she came upstairs. "Hi, Honey. I didn't even hear you drive in. How was your day?"

She dropped her supplies in the farmhouse sink and turned on the water. Adam had set his Yeti cup on the counter next to her. *Why can't he put this in the dishwasher?* She loaded it into the dishwasher with the other dirty dishes. He'd want his favorite mug ready for tomorrow. Every morning she handed him his coffee before he left, making it exactly how he liked it for his drive to one of his three real estate offices.

"It was fine." He stood in the middle of the kitchen, flipping through the mail, ignoring Cora, who sat at his feet, waiting for some attention. "I'm beat. Everyone wants a home that's move-in ready." His thick, dark hair was longer than usual, and he hadn't shaved for a few days.

He set the mail down on the island and let out a sigh. "This new office in New Hampshire is gonna be the death of me." He rubbed his eyes with the heel of his hands, then peeled off his jacket and dropped it on the island.

Rachel had warned him of this when he'd told her he wanted to tap into the Southern Maine and New Hampshire market, but he'd told her she didn't know what she was talking about, and she needed to let him handle it.

He slowly headed to the living room and plopped down in the black leather Eames chair and stared at the blank sixty inch television that hung over the fireplace.

Rachel had loved the completely open first floor when the kids were younger. She'd painted the trim a light gray and the walls a creamy shade of white. It was bright and tranquil, and she'd loved watching them play with their toys on the plush throw rug on the livingroom floor as she baked in the kitchen.

But now, a few walls wouldn't be so bad.

"I'm beat too," Rachel said, squeezing water from her brushes and sponge. "My sore throat is getting worse. Maybe you can help make dinner?"

He'd been busy and stressed out with the opening of the New Hampshire office, and she hadn't been asking much of him lately. But she was exhausted too and genuinely felt like shit.

"You're sick?" Adam asked, clicking on the television, turning the volume up to sixty.

Rachel closed her eyes as hot resentment rose in her chest. "I told you this morning before you left, I felt like I was coming down with something." She picked up his jacket, about to go through the motions of hanging it in the closet like she always did, then thought better of it and threw it back down on the island.

She already had two children. Should she have to pick up after a man-child too?

"Oh, right." He nodded his head, eyes locked on the basketball game. "I'll help as soon as this quarter ends." He moved to the edge of the chair. "Jesus! It's like they don't even know what defense is!" He glanced at Rachel distractedly. "Have a Diet Coke, hon, that always makes you feel better."

Rachel slammed the packet of chicken on the counter. She could ask the kids. *No. They've been in school all day and just finished their homework. Just do it yourself.*

Once the chicken was popping and sizzling in the oven, Rachel started a pot of rice, then got out all the fixings for a salad and started chopping.

Adam was still laser-focused on the game, now leaned back in the Eames chair, one khaki-clad leg crossed over the other. Rachel narrowed her eyes at him. *You shouldn't have to ask him again. You shouldn't have to ask in the first place.*

She pushed the thought away and set her knife aside before digging her phone out of her purse to text Joanna and let her know her mother's painting was ready to be picked up.

While her phone was in her hand, *another* email from Benjamin's science teacher came through. Apparently, he'd been late three times this quarter and was often "disruptive in class." *Not again.* A knot of worry clung to her chest.

Have Adam talk to him after dinner. You aren't getting through to him.

She returned to cutting up the tomatoes, peppers, and carrots, throwing everything over the bed of lettuce and then getting out all their salad dressings.

She took a deep breath before entering the living room to interrupt Adam's game. "Dinner is ready. Can you call the kids?"

"Sure," he said, his eyes not leaving the television. "Benny, Elsa, dinner!" he yelled.

Rachel returned to the kitchen, got out the black cloth napkins, and folded them in half before tucking them under the new black silverware she'd just bought. There was something about setting a nice table that relaxed her.

Adam shuffled to the kitchen. "I'm sorry, I said I'd help. You should have said something!"

"I did say something. I shouldn't have to beg for help from my husband," she whispered between clenched teeth, worried the kids would hear. "I'm sick of asking you the same thing over and over. Not to mention I'm *literally sick*."

She rolled her eyes as he observed the set table.

"Can you please turn off the television?" she asked, spooning the rice from its pot into a bowl, setting it next to the platter of chicken on the table.

The kids came down, and everyone took their seats.

"Finish your math?" she asked Benjamin as he piled chicken onto his plate.

"Yup!"

"Good job. And you need to get it together for science class. I just heard from your teacher. *Again*."

"K," Benjamin said, stabbing an uncut piece of chicken with his fork before taking a bite.

Rachel watched him and sighed. "We have knives, you know."

"Too much work," Benjamin said, bringing the chicken to his mouth again.

Adam raised his eyebrows.

Rachel leaned closer to Adam. "I heard from Mr. Miller again. He's still coming to class late and messing around." They both looked over at Benjamin, who was still gnawing at the colossal piece of chicken hanging from his fork. "Can you *please* have a talk with him after dinner? I'm tired of these emails, and my words don't seem to sink in."

"Sure," Adam said. He turned to Elsa. "How was your day, beautiful girl?" He took her phone and put it down on the other side of his plate, where she couldn't reach it.

"It was good." She rolled her eyes and let out a sigh, glancing longingly at her phone.

"You know the rules. You can have it back after dinner." Adam bit into his chicken, then looked down at his plate. "Didn't you put the usual seasoning on this tonight?" He grabbed the salt and shook it over his plate. "It's much better like that."

His dark hair was graying at the temples, and his blue eyes were bloodshot. The scowl on his face made him look like an overgrown, bratty teenager who wasn't getting his way.

"No, we were out of teriyaki marinade and I forgot to get more while I was at the grocery store yesterday. It's fine like this."

Rachel pressed her thumb into the edge of their dark antique dining table as she watched her husband wrinkle his nose and chew on his chicken. He swallowed hard, and her toes curled as she listened to him dig food out of his teeth with his tongue.

He'd unbuttoned his dress shirt, and his salt-and-pepper chest hair was peeking out, reminding her of an old rug. The lines between his eyes were deep, and he scrunched his face up the same way it always was when they'd argue about the lack of sex in their marriage. Which was often.

Rachel felt Elsa watching her and straightened herself up in her chair.

"What are you guys going to do for Halloween this year? Want to have a party with your friends like last year?"

Both kids lit up at the suggestion. "I think this year we should put a bunch of different slimy, nasty things in buckets with lids. Make people put their hands in them and guess what they are," Elsa suggested.

"Yeah, like slime, worms, and cold oatmeal!" Benjamin chimed in, his mouth full of meat.

As the kids hatched their plans, Rachel concentrated on *not* shooting disapproving looks at her husband. When

Benjamin and Elsa picked up on the tension in their marriage, which was pretty thick lately, it killed Rachel.

After dinner, Rachel hugged both kids, turning her face away so she wouldn't breathe on them and get them sick. "I'm headed up to bed. I'm exhausted."

Upstairs, she washed her face and brushed her teeth, but skipped applying her retinol and didn't do her nightly Gua Sha ritual.

She sank into their king-sized bed, pulled the plump down comforter up to her chin, and stuffed two tissues in her nostrils. After a few minutes of watching HGTV, she fell into a deep sleep.

∿

Hours later, the sound of Adam's electric toothbrush woke her up. One tissue had fallen out of her nose onto the bed, and she picked it up and put it on her nightstand. "Did you talk to Benny?" she whispered, as Adam crawled into bed.

"Yeah. He'll be fine. Just a stage." Adam rolled toward her, slowly rubbing her arm. His breathing hitched, and Rachel's shoulders stiffened to her ears.

"I hope so. I just don't want it to get worse. He's too old to act like this," she said through a yawn. *He must know you're too worn out for sex right now.*

"Don't stress, Rachel. It'll be fine." His hand made its way up to her jawline, and he traced his thumb down her neck, the pressure hurting her swollen throat.

Did he touch that other woman this way?

Nausea swam in her gut. "Adam, please. You know I'm not feeling well. Maybe tomorrow." Rachel rolled onto her other side. It *had* been a *really* long time. But even if she wasn't feeling shitty, the fact that he hadn't helped her with dinner, and his display about the chicken, was enough to turn her off for a while. They'd had so many talks like this since Elsa had been born, and it seemed to be white noise to Adam.

He let out a long sigh and slapped his hands down on the bed. "Rachel. It's been like five months." Cora's head popped up from the foot of the bed, and she scooted closer to Rachel, as if choosing sides. *Good girl.*

Rachel clenched her eyes shut and took in a long breath. "Okay, it's been a while. But I am feeling awful tonight. I'm sure tomorrow night I'll feel better and we can—"

"You're always happy once we do it, Honey." His tone was gentler now. "You need to ... try. It's like you don't even try anymore." He propped his head up with his elbow, his silhouette backlit by the plug-in nightlight on the wall behind him. She'd been so attracted to him once, and could tell when they were in public that other women found him attractive. *You can get it back.*

Adam kissed her mouth and then her neck. She held in her squirms and the urge to shout, "Stop touching me!" Instead, she took in a sharp breath and whispered, "Not tonight, Adam. Tomorrow. I promise."

Adam rolled over on his side so his back was to her. "You always have some freaking excuse, Rachel. Whatever."

During sex and fights about their lack of intimacy, she wondered if he had continued cheating on her since the affair ten years ago. *If you hadn't caught him, would he have told you? If you had a higher sex drive, would your life be different? Was his affair your fault? How would you feel if he never wanted to have sex with you?*

He'd said it was just the one time, a horrible slipup. And she'd believed him. But she also never would have believed he'd hurt her the way he did. She'd married Adam because he'd made her feel safe. But then, his affair took that safety away.

Rachel stared at the back of his head, half relieved and half filled with dread, knowing she'd have to make good on her promise tomorrow night. But was that really so terrible?

He still wants to have sex with you, even though you have snot and tissues coming out of your nose. It could be so much worse.

She thought about the look Elsa had given her at dinner. It made her want to try harder for them. "Tomorrow night," she whispered. "I promise."

**Get *Before She Knew* on
http://katiebinghamsmith.com.**

About the Author

Katie Bingham-Smith earned her BA in English and writes full-time from her home in Maine with her three kids, two ducks, and Goldendoodle. When she's not writing steamy, small-town romance novels, you can find her redecorating her home, sucking back a Coke Zero with her nose in a book, or at the gym.

Stay up to date on all her latest book news on katiebinghamsmith.com.

Made in the USA
Middletown, DE
03 July 2024